TREEHOUSE HOTEL
COZY MYSTERIES

Books 1 – 3

Peonies and Peril

Violets and Vengeance

Buttercups and Betrayal

Sue Hollowell

A Treehouse Hotel Cozy Mystery Collection Book 1 – 3

PEONIES AND PERIL

A TREEHOUSE HOTEL COZY MYSTERY (BOOK 1)

SUE HOLLOWELL

CHAPTER ONE

Mom kept the books for the Cedarbrook Treehouse Hotel on a shelf along one wall. There were six bookcases with stacks of grid-lined paper journals. At least she had the sense to put a date on the front of each one. Trouble was, I had no idea what the date represented. But it was a start. Mom, Brittany, and I hunkered down in the office of the hotel, attempting to excavate any sense of order to the bookkeeping for the business.

"Mom, why didn't you ever get with the twenty-first century and use a computer? These books are a mess. I can't even discern the basics of income and expenses. For example, what's 'tomorrow's baby'?"

"Chloe, you were always such a worrywart. Don't stress. I've been doing fine since Marty died and we still sometimes have guests."

"I'm not a worrywart, huh, boy?" My faithful companion looked up at me with big brown eyes.

"What was that, dear?" my mother questioned.

"Nothing, Mom. Just talking to Max."

"You and that dog. You'd think you were best friends." My gaze met Max's in perfect understanding. He shrugged, and I sighed.

My head hurt and it was only 9:00 a.m. Unraveling the mess of books for this place would take a while. It was such a beautiful place. You felt like you'd gone back in time to your childhood. Who wouldn't love staying in a treehouse? Most units had basic plumbing, some had heat. Each one was raised above the ground. You reached most places either through stairs or one even had a suspension bridge. No TVs. Each treehouse was on the edge of a central gathering area where you could have a campfire. If you closed your eyes when you were inside, you felt like you were the last person on the planet. Their names reflected local agricultural items: Crabapple Chalet, Buttercup Bungalow, Cherry Cottage, Morning Glory Manor, Snowberry Sanctuary, and Huckleberry Hut. The fact the place had deteriorated under Mom's watch was not her fault. I just hoped I could help make it financially attractive to a buyer. I like a good number puzzle, but this was a doozy. Unlike any sudoku I'd ever mastered.

"Why didn't you at least hire an accountant? I'm shocked the IRS hasn't descended and confiscated every asset you have."

"I did, Chloe. I hired Walter on Sandy's recommendation. He did the accounting for the Garden Club for a while, but he turned out to be a loser, so Edna fired him too."

I couldn't tell if the place was salvageable or if I'd have to start over. That alone diverted my brain to a huckleberry vodka. But I'd wait until at least afternoon so I didn't endure Mom's wrath. Or maybe I wouldn't. I'd get the wrath for something or other, might as well make it something I'd enjoy.

"Seriously, Mom. I don't know if I can fix this. You might just have to sell the hotel so someone with experience in these things can come in and do it the right way."

"Chloe, no! We can't sell. I'm sure you can handle it. You are an accountant, right? So we're good."

Chloe the fixer. Always the one to get everyone out of a jam. Here's an idea - don't get into the jam in the first place. The weight of returning home pressed down on my chest. I missed my own space. The distance between me and my family. My own identity, separate from these crazy people. Taking care of others had always fallen to me. I was the oldest of four kids. But only by a few minutes. My sisters Zoe, Joey, and I were triplets. No doubt we were a massive handful for Mom. I never had kids, so I can't even imagine one, let alone three at once. And if that weren't enough, baby brother Harrison came along a year later. The fact we were all alive was probably a feat in itself for Mom.

Mom had her own drama. Seven husbands. Maybe she kept going until lucky number seven. It turned out to be true. Marty was a gem. Frankly, I don't know what he saw in Mom. Four kids, six prior husbands, kind of a train wreck. But somehow they made it work. Marty seemed to get Mom. He brought out the best in her. For all of my life, her time with Marty made her the happiest. Not gonna lie, when they married I was skeptical. Mostly on Marty's behalf. I sure missed him. When he passed with no kids, the hotel became Mom's. I don't know how she kept it going for all these years.

"Brittany, do you understand the system?" I asked.

"Aunt Chloe, I just do what your Mom asks. We have these enormous books here where I write when someone makes a reservation and the amount they will pay. Then when I get a bill, I write a check and write that amount down next to it."

Heavens to mergatroyd, my head's going to explode! I took a cleansing, deep breath. *How am I ever going to get through this? And it's no good arguing with Mom. She's got her own revisionist history.*

"OK, I think I'll take the most recent book and start from the beginning. Mom, what time do you need to be at Caroline's for the Garden Club meeting?"

"Eleven o'clock."

I swear, an inch of dust covered the books. One spark and this whole place would explode in an inferno. I'd only been back a month, but it seemed like I'd never left. I loved my Mom. She had a hard life and did the best she could. I knew that. But I wanted to enjoy my retirement and keep my distance for the life I'd built.

ele

If I could shape up this place to be more presentable, I'd only help my cause. I was a bit rusty at DIY projects, but maybe I'd have to break out my old tool belt. Frank and I had enjoyed remodeling in our spare time. I missed those times terribly with my husband. His passing was so sudden. The 1950s house we bought looked nothing like it did when we first moved in.

In the meantime, I cracked open the first book. Line one, Davenport family— $297.24. OK, that seems straightforward. Line two, Edges— $12.98. For all of my education and experience as an accountant, I'd never seen anything like this. And I'd worked for some doozies of a company. Maybe having all of this go up in flames wasn't a bad idea after all.

"Mom or Brittany, what is Edges for $12.98?"

They looked at each other and shrugged.

"Is it a company?" I asked. "Is it a product? It can't be a guest. It's too small of an amount."

"Sorry, Aunt Chloe. Doesn't ring a bell."

My phone buzzed. The sound rescued me from this accounting nightmare. Caroline was calling, saving me from the number jungle, for now.

"Hi Caroline, what's up?" Caroline was a high school friend. Pretty much everyone in this town could claim that mantle. When you grew up in a town of about two thousand, everyone was more like extended family, and they all knew your business.

"Chloe, it's Edna!" she yelled into the phone, causing me to extend it from my ear.

"What? Isn't this Caroline?" I asked. Mom and Brittany were now engrossed from hearing my side of the conversation.

"Chloe, yes. This is me, Caroline. I'm at Edna's."

"Caroline. What's happening? Are you OK?"

7

"I am. But Edna's not. I came by to pick her up for the Garden Club meeting. You know we're having elections today. I wanted to be nice to her because I'm sure nobody will vote to keep her president. I mean, she has that ridiculous platform to beautify the town by—"

"Caroline, what's going on?"

The rivalry between those two ran deep. All the way back to school. Always competing any way they could, especially for boys. Edna won in that category. Her boyfriend previously dated Caroline. And Edna never let Caroline forget it. Max stood. His big droopy ears swayed as he meandered over to me. He stared, imparting empathy.

"When I got here and rang the bell, there was no answer. The front door was open and just the screen door was closed. I yelled for Edna. Because, you know, she's so private I didn't want to just barge in."

"Caroline, spit it out. What's going on?"

"Edna's dead." I looked at Mom, not wanting to repeat what I just heard.

"How do you know? Where is she?"

Mom, Brittany, and Max were all now on alert that something was not right at the other end of that phone line.

"Oh, Chloe." Caroline blubbered so hard I couldn't understand a word. I needed her to calm down without alarming everyone else and creating a panic I couldn't control.

"Caroline. Breathe and tell me where she is."

"Chloe, what's happening?" Mom now joined the panic party. "Is Edna all right? Chloe!"

"Chloe, she's facedown in her garden. It looks like she's just sleeping. I yelled at her and shook her and no response. I touched her." Caroline lost it and sobbed so hard I figured we were done. Plus, I got the gist.

"Caroline, is Ralph there?" Silence. "Caroline. Listen to me." She mumbled something close enough to concurrence. "Go inside the house, drink some water, and sit down. We'll be there soon. Can you do that?" More mumbling.

I disconnected the call. Mom and Brittany sprang up. Max sprinted toward the door. Road trip to Edna's. And another opportunity to hang his head out the window where his long fur blew like he was Farrah Fawcett at a photo shoot. Well, this wasn't the diversion I would have asked for from my accounting job of a lifetime. I had to admit, Spokane wasn't dull, but it was my life, my choices. Somehow in Cedarbrook, drama swirled like tornadoes on a regular basis, sweeping up everyone in its path. No life untouched. It was barely 9:30 a.m. on a Monday. If deciphering the hotel books wasn't enough of a puzzle to solve, now we had a death.

CHAPTER TWO

The drive to Edna's took about ten minutes. Every trip in this town took about ten minutes.

"Chloe, are you going to tell me what's going on?" Mom asked.

I couldn't keep it quiet much longer. She'd figure it out when we arrived and saw Edna splayed in her back yard.

"Caroline said something's wrong with Edna. She got there and couldn't find her, so she went to her garden."

"Did she have a heart attack? I knew it. I kept telling her not eat so much of that red meat. It seemed like every day she was at that Smokehouse Restaurant scarfing down steak. I knew it'd get her. Wait 'til I give her a piece of my mind. She never listened when I was married to her dad, either." Lloyd was Edna's dad, Mom's husband number three. She tried to mother Edna as a teenager and that didn't go well.

I had to let the cat out of the bag before we got there. Caroline was hysterical enough. I couldn't be outnumbered with runaway emotions. Even with Max the Calmer by my side, it'd still be too much to tackle.

"Mom, it looks like Edna's dead."

She gave me a pointed look. "Chloe, stop joking. I'm sure Caroline was just being dramatic. Or you misunderstood. You know Caroline and Edna both want to be Garden Club president. And we're having the election today. Caroline will do anything to oust Edna. She's never gotten over the defeat."

"Mom, I'm serious. Caroline said she found her face down in her backyard," I whispered.

Saying it any louder felt like it would make it come true. I glanced at Mom in the front passenger seat. Her face stoic. That woman had seen a fair amount of death in her lifetime, more than most.

"But, Chloe. It can't be. Maybe she just fell and passed out."

I pulled into the cul-de-sac, circling counterclockwise to park on the street just before Edna's house. Caroline's Cadillac filled the driveway. Mom sprang from the car with the energy of someone forty years her junior. Physically, she was still in pretty amazing shape. Mentally she was obviously aging. Max and I quickly exited and caught up with her. Edna's dog Trixie barked with the veracity of a Doberman. That little Cavalier King Charles spaniel was too adorable to harm a fly.

"Mom, hang on. Let's go find Caroline first."

She complied.

We approached the screen door and I could see through it that Caroline had followed my instructions. The door squeaked as I slowly pushed it aside. Mom and Max followed me in. The door slammed behind us and jolted Caroline. Her head snapped in our direction with tears streaked down her face.

"Oh, Mabel. I can't believe she's gone. Poor Edna," Caroline moaned.

Max pushed his way to the front and rested his head on Caroline's knee. She lifted a hand from the water glass and placed it on his head. No tail wagging for now. Somehow, he knew this was not a happy visit. Trixie mirrored his actions and sat by his side with her head on Caroline's foot.

"Mom, you stay here with Caroline." Further obedience without a peep. I left the both of them in Max's capable paws and headed to a bedroom to find a blanket. I pulled the comforter off of a bed in the spare room and used the hallway through the kitchen to the backyard.

Yep, there she was.

Face down in her prized peonies. I gently covered her as if she were taking an afternoon nap. I'd never seen a dead body up close and personal. Frank had relayed stories from his time on the force, but there was nothing like a front row seat.

"Hi, Chloe." I jumped, almost falling myself.

Max and Trixie sped around the yard, figurines falling like dominoes. They stopped to observe and sniff Edna. And after a quick pit stop, resumed their romping and chasing crows. I shuffled them safely back inside.

"Sorry, should have shut the door," said Buzz, who I'd called before I left the hotel.

"It's OK, Buzz. We're all understandably distracted. Sorry to bother you on the golf course." Buzz was a retired cop from our town. But today, I was thankful he agreed to come.

"Where's Ralph?" Buzz asked.

"He went to pick up car parts in Emerald Hills."

"Oh yeah. The Studebaker's gone." Buzz worked his way along the garden path, winding past the yard art, figurines and jungle of flowers and shrubs. "Dang, I really hoped someone was mistaken. Or at least pulling my leg, as cruel a joke that would be."

Sunflowers were everywhere, as if seeds had been sprayed from a hose. They were pretty cute but didn't seem to fit the design and tone of the fancier garden. Edna's garden was one of her prized possessions. She won awards every year for many of her flowers. The hotel sure could have used her touch with designing beautiful garden spaces.

"I'm afraid not. I wonder what happened. Mom said Edna's diet could have caused a heart attack, maybe that's it."

Buzz circled the body, an experienced law enforcement officer keenly eying clues.

"Not sure. It looks like she possibly tripped over something. But that shouldn't cause a death by itself. Some of the peonies appear trampled. And these morning glory vines look like they could reach out and trip you. What is that glass ball over there?"

Buzz referred to a gazing globe that normally would have been situated on a display stand. The blue-swirled orb now sat shattered about eight feet from Edna's head, the stand on its side.

"That's a gazing globe, a garden decoration."

"A what?" Buzz knelt down and examined the pieces of the globe. "You ladies and your garden things. Well, maybe she tripped on the vines and hit her head on it. I see a bump the size of a golf ball near her ear."

"Buzz, what do we do now?"

"I'll call over to Emerald Hills PD and have them take it from here. Hmmph."

"Buzz, what are you thinking? This was an accident, right?"

Buzz and I went way back. It had been over forty years since I'd spent any real time with him. We were such confidants back then, sharing our dreams and our woes. When we dated in high school, that nonverbal communication style drove me nuts. I was a very concrete person. Just say what you're thinking and not all of those other guttural sounds I was supposed to translate.

"Well, Chloe. I think so. But frankly, from the position she's laying, the tripping and hitting her head don't line up with the truth. Just best to have the pros take a gander."

This was horrible. Edna wasn't the most likable person, but her death would send shock waves through the town. I headed inside to see what mess I'd have to clean up there.

Max and Trixie had returned to their duty station at Caroline's side. Thankfully, they followed directions, unlike Mom. She was nowhere to be found. I searched the house to no avail. Maybe she returned to the car, not wanting to be anywhere near death. I headed to the driveway. She was on the phone, pacing. She spotted me and gave a little wave.

"Mom, we need to go."

She stopped in her tracks and stared at me.

"Mom!" That earned me a dirty look. She had a handful of tissues stopping up her tears and sniffles.

"You know, Pearl, I didn't like her either, but I'd certainly never wish her dead. I mean Edna was such a pill when I was married to her father. But I did have a soft spot for her too. Pearl, I have to go. I'll see you in a bit." She hung up the phone.

I planted my hands on my hips. "What are you doing talking to Pearl? I hope you didn't tell her what's going on. We need to leave that to the authorities. It's not our place."

"Chloe, are you kidding me?" Mom shook her head and stomped toward me. "Of course I called Pearl. First of all, she's Buzz's wife so she'll know soon enough anyway. Plus, I wanted her to know we need to find another person to run against Caroline for the Garden Club president and wanted to see if maybe she would do it. I mean, just because Edna's gone doesn't mean Caroline should get the position free and clear."

You always chose a side in this town. And Mom was definitely on Team Edna.

"Mom, I'm sure that's the last thing on Caroline's mind right now. I'm going back inside to get the dogs and we'll head back to the hotel. I'm sure by now Brittany could use some help."

She followed my return to the house and through the slamming screen door. Buzz had joined Caroline. She hadn't moved a muscle. Max and Trixie stood guard as if Caroline was president and they were the secret service. I searched the kitchen and utility room to gather Trixie's food, leash, and dog bed. When I returned to the living room, Mom sat next to Caroline with her hand on her back, consoling her.

"Chloe, I called the Emerald Hills guys," Buzz said. "They're on their way. I'll wait here so you guys can go."

"Chloe," my mom said. "We can't leave until we find out what happened to Edna. Why don't you stay here and help? I'll go with Caroline to the Garden Club meeting."

We froze.

"Yes, Mabel's right." Caroline had come out of her stupor and back to the conscious world. "I think having the election would be what Edna would have wanted."

"I agree, Caroline." Mom gave me a sharp look. "Besides, Chloe. You're one of the smartest people I know. I mean, you're helping me straighten out the books at the hotel. That's kind of like being a detective, in a way."

Now she'd really lost it. "That's ridiculous. I'd just be in the way. The pros have this handled. Besides, I need to take care of the dogs."

A quick glance down showed Trixie and Max patiently waiting for my next move.

"Well, look how well-behaved they are. They'll be fine with us. You don't mind them coming to your store, do you, Caroline?"

I was pretty sure with the way Caroline's mouth turned to a frown that she did mind. But her diversion of the election gave her a free and clear path to become the Garden Club president.

I shook my head. "I'm not staying. But Buzz? Can you give me a call later with an update?"

That appeased Mom. Pretty sure this day couldn't get worse. Digging through those hotel financial journals, and poor Edna's death. The story was that she was a gruff, difficult woman to deal with. She didn't have it easy growing up. Her Mom left her when she was young. Over time, her behavior resembled the classic eccentric old woman. She wouldn't harm a fly but was the kind of person that gave off a vibe you either liked or you didn't. People didn't understand what Ralph saw in her. Beauty was in the eye of the beholder. I truly believed there was someone on the planet to love every person. Edna wasn't afraid to speak her mind. That got her into some hefty disagreements on a regular basis. I really hoped that had nothing to do with her death.

"Plus, we have an election to conduct," Caroline mumbled to herself as she zipped out the door and sped away from the quiet cul-de-sac.

Did Caroline seriously just say that? How could she even think of having the Garden Club election today?

Mom didn't seem to notice as she led us silently out of the house, with me and the dogs bringing up the rear. Max and Trixie bounced along as they saw they were going for a ride. I wished my outlook could change on a dime like a dog's does. One minute extremely somber, then the next, prancing down the walk for that ultimate road trip. I held the back door of my car open. The dogs bounded in. I tossed Trixie's supplies in the back and we headed to Caroline's. What new uproar was in store for us there?

CHAPTER THREE

Max and Trixie jockeyed for the open spot to see through to the front seat. "Knock it off, you two. Good manners or I'll take you home." Right. Max had me wrapped around his puppy paw since I had adopted him at six weeks. My rescue Cocker Spaniel had the sensitivity of a psychic and seemed to know my thoughts and feelings before I did. He melted my heart with his compassionate, large brown, warm eyes. His buff-colored, long fur, and droopy ears exuded a regal look. Trixie was a whole other story. She was like the pesky little sister. A stinker, but cute as a bug. Her chestnut and white body wiggled even more wildly than Max's did when she wagged her tail.

We pulled into the small parking lot at Caroline's Confections. The two-story building looked the same as the day it was built in the 1950s. The brick-lined flowerbed that hugged the building held sad little multi-colored geraniums. How could a member of the Garden Club accept that with a straight face? Especially one who wanted to be president of those wacky women? Caroline rented out the upper floor to a young couple for additional income.

"Mom, wait here while I get the dogs' leashes." I got out of the car and went to the back, where they both just about leapt out of the car before I slammed the hatch.

"Chloe, why don't you go back to the hotel? I can call you when we're done."

With the pups leading the way and straining my arm, I entered the store. "I'm fine, Mom. Let's just see how it goes."

"Don't say I didn't warn you."

Mom and I wound our way through the loads of stuff Caroline had for sale. One might call it crap. Her coffee shop had turned into a hodgepodge where the confections seemed to be an afterthought. It was as if any old idea about what to sell made its way into this place. We navigated through the miniature doll display, the hanging plants, and the hat rack, to an opening behind the bakery counter. A small room with tables, chairs, and no windows had become the meeting place for the Garden Club. Initially, Caroline had offered the space for free, but now charged a small fee for its use. She was running a business, not a charity. I heard the chatter before we entered the room. Max had stopped to smell a tray of gingerbread cookies cooling on a side table. His sweet tooth ruled him again. He sat on his haunches and gazed at me for approval. *Not now, buddy.* I gently tugged and we went into the room.

Caroline was holding court. The place was full, and it wasn't even time for the meeting to start. I heard low mumbles and Edna's name. In a town of this size, when you sneeze, the people on the other side of the street say 'bless you'. Literally nothing was a secret. The more you tried to keep something on the down low, the more likely it got out.

"Caroline, you must be traumatized after seeing that," Sandy said. She was forever trying to get into Caroline's good graces. From the dawn of time, Sandy attempted entry into Caroline's clique. For a time, Caroline would temporarily admit her, only to shun her.

"Oh, Sandy. I can't even begin to tell you how horrible it was," Caroline moaned. "And poor Edna was up for Garden Club president re-election. And there she was, lying dead in her own garden. Well, maybe that was a fitting way for her to go." Gasps echoed throughout the room. Mom sniffed.

"I bet she ate some of those peonies," Loretta said, wiping her eyes. "She was always making those salads with her flowers and she probably mistook the poison ones. Did the cops say what happened?"

"Let's not speculate," I said. "We need to wait for the medical examiner's report." All heads turned toward me, Mom, and the dogs. The four of us joined a table in the corner.

"Hi Chloe, so nice to see you. Hi Mabel. Is that Edna's dog?" Sandy asked.

"Yes, for now I'm keeping her. She'll be a nice playmate for Max until we find her a new home. I know Ralph never wanted her in the first place."

Trixie yipped. Sandy jumped. "Well, keep her away from me. She seems vicious. Every time I was at Edna's she mauled me."

Trixie yipped again. *I agree, girl. Sandy can be a lot to take in.* Max sidled next to Trixie, his stubby tail pointed straight back, ears cocked forward. His demeanor confirmed suspicions that Sandy was not a dog person. And why would she be at Edna's? She didn't even like her.

"Wait," Sandy continued. "What if it wasn't an accident after all?"

"Whoa." I raised my hands. "Please, let's wait for the report. I'll call Buzz to get an update and you'll all be the first to know." Give 'em what they want. First in line for gossip.

"Well, maybe I should just talk to Buzz myself, then," Sandy snipped. She wouldn't let this go. "You know, Edna and Ralph argued all the time. He's such a hothead. The last time they were at the Smokehouse, they were going at it again."

"About what? Where is he anyway?" Loretta chimed in.

"Chloe's right." All heads swiveled toward Caroline. "Let's wait for the authorities to do their thing and we'll get on with our meeting. I mean, I'm sure Edna would want us to carry on with the election. You all know how important this club was to her."

Some heads nodded. More mumbles disagreed about proceeding.

Max and Trixie settled on the floor, watching the goings on like a tennis match. Eyes darted from one speaker to the next, ready to bound when anyone made a move. Caroline stood and went to the podium. The dogs jumped to attention. Max's ears lurched forward again. His instinct for people was spot on and he sensed something about Caroline wasn't quite what it seemed. He peeked an eye toward me, ensuring I was fully aware of the concern.

"On behalf of Edna," Caroline said, "I'd like to call the meeting to order."

"Caroline, I just think it's shameful of us to carry on as if nothing has happened," Mom said. "Shouldn't we wait an appropriate amount of time? Chloe, how much time should we wait after someone dies before we have our meeting?"

"Mom, I don't know. We're all here. And there's nothing we can do right now. I agree with Caroline. Edna would have wanted us to carry on. She cared a lot about the work this group does."

Caroline grinned, appearing confident in her victory.

CHAPTER FOUR

The packed house sat in rapt attention. This would be the talk of the town for the foreseeable future. An unexplained death and the gall to proceed with an election that same day.

"I couldn't agree more, Chloe. OK. First order of business is reading of last meeting's minutes." Caroline behaved as if she'd already been elected. "Loretta, would you please do the honors? And seriously, we need to elect an official secretary and treasurer. The willy-nilly record keeping of Edna's was atrocious. Who knows what shape the club is really in? When she fired Walter, that was the last straw for me." Caroline was in full-on campaigning mode. "I just can't." Loretta sniffled. "It's too soon. We're dishonoring Edna. I don't know how you can stand up there as if nothing has happened. It's heartless." Loretta continued into a blubber.

"She's right, Caroline." Pearl patted Loretta's back, joining Team Edna. "Let's postpone for a week. At least until we say a proper goodbye to Edna."

Max lifted his head and squinted intensely at me. His eyes inquired about the rising tension in the room. I reached over and gave him a reassuring pat. Trixie stood, inching as close to Max as possible, and plopped her body right on top of him. As if to say, you pet him, you must pet me too. What a diva. He tipped his head down toward her and raised his eyebrows. *Really, girl?*

"Chloe's logic makes sense. How about we have the election and then close the meeting early?" Caroline wouldn't let this go until she had her way. "I'd like to share my plans for the club. Then if anyone else wants to get into the running for the position, you can go next." Without the boldness of Edna, I had no idea who'd be brave enough to challenge Caroline.

"Well, I guess I could," Pearl said.

Caroline's shoulders deflated. I'm sure she had hoped for an uncontested election. Likely with Edna as an opponent she wouldn't have won. "OK. Here we go." Caroline gripped the podium with both hands like she was trying to keep it from toppling over. Her knuckles whitened.

"Ladies of the Garden Club." She was going all out with a show. Drama in this little club rivaled a Broadway production. "I'd like to share with you today my plans to take the work we do to new heights. To make this club the envy of the county. To make more money than we ever have in the past." There it was. Caroline's focus never strayed far from the almighty buck. Her family had owned the bakery for many years. But it looked exactly the same as it had for generations. There were more things for sale than bakery items, making me question what business she was really in. If she had such a brilliant business mind, why had the place continued to look as if it would fall apart any day? Rumors swirled about financial troubles. Caroline finished her stump speech, paused, and took in the smattering of claps. She took a seat in the front row, a smug smile on her face, as Pearl made her way to the podium. Pearl would be a great president. From a business perspective, she appeared to have it much more together than Caroline. Pearl's Pooch Pampering was a thriving business, even in this tiny town. People spent a ton of money on their dogs. She had customers from all over the county.

"First, let me say, I wouldn't be doing this if Edna were still alive. I really just want to be able to carry on her legacy. We are a garden club and Edna was all about the plants. Sure, we made some money and we need that to operate. But first and foremost, I believe our agricultural focus should remain, just as Edna would have wanted." Pearl nailed it.

I didn't know she had this in her. Despite her reluctance to pursue the position I was sure she'd sway some votes to her side.

"That's right, Pearl," Mom cheered her on.

"Mom," I whispered.

"What?" she replied. "Pearl's right."

"Mabel, let her finish. Then we can take our vote." Caroline huffed and rolled her eyes.

"I think that's all I need to say. Thank you." A similar smattering of claps for Pearl sounded throughout the room.

Caroline leapt to the podium, resuming charge. Low chatter began at each table. "OK, everyone. Now it's time to vote. At each table are pens and slips of paper. Write down your vote and put your paper in the box up here. Chloe, we need a neutral party to count the votes. Would you do that?"

I'd hoped to be a fly on the wall here. But now I was smack dab in the center. "Sure. Mom, can you hold the leashes to keep these two in check?"

One by one, each Garden Club member approached the ballot box and deposited her vote. If Caroline didn't win, we'd hear no end to it. For that reason alone, I cared just that much for her to be the victor.

Sandy was the last to cast her vote. Averting her eyes, she took her seat. The room full of women was eerily silent. I took a piece of paper and pen from the podium to tally the votes. I made two columns and labeled each with the name of the candidate. I opened the box and set the top aside. I retrieved the first, a folded piece of paper.

"One vote for Pearl." I entered a tally mark in Pearl's column. I retrieved paper number two, slowly and obviously for all to see. "One vote for Pearl." Another tally mark. From the corner of my eye, I could see Caroline in the front row slump just a little in her seat. She was probably counting bodies in the room to calculate the number to win. I retrieved another ballot. "One vote for Caroline." She raised back up to a full-seated height. There were eight more votes, the total an odd number. We'd have a winner today. I continued my announcements, adding votes neck and neck for Pearl and Caroline. Ten counted, one to go. I looked in the box to confirm the final piece of paper. "The last vote goes to—" I swear I heard a gasp. "Caroline. Congratulations."

She flew out of her seat and to the podium in two steps, nudging me aside with a snide look. I returned to my table and was greeted like royalty from the pups. Unconditional love.

"Well, as your new president we have lots of work to do. First off—"

"Wait, I thought we were postponing any business until after the election to—" Loretta interjected.

"What I was trying to say before the interruption is that I think we should honor Edna in some way." Caroline forged ahead as if she'd been waiting for this moment forever. "I have lots of ideas. What I want to do is name a scholarship after her for students who will study agriculture in college."

"I think that's something we should vote on," Sandy said. Caroline's ally questioned her actions. If looks could kill, we'd have two dead club members. Yikes! This wasn't just for fun, it was serious business.

"We don't need a vote." Caroline glared at her. "Let's just do it. I mean, who could dispute that it represents Edna well?"

No one wanted to argue, so Caroline achieved her second triumph in a mere ten minutes. Silence enveloped the room. Caroline gaveled the meeting to an end, the sound echoing. I led the way with the pups to escape the awkwardness and stifling air closing in. I couldn't get out of there fast enough. *Note to self. Next time, just drop Mom off at the meeting.*

CHAPTER FIVE

M om and I had stopped for coffee before joining Brittany at the hotel for another day digging into the hotel books. I was so torn about staying at Mom's during my visit. With my plan to only be here six months or so, it didn't make sense to get my own place. Mom, Max, Trixie, and I arrived early to continue the scavenger hunt for a glimmer of organization in how the hotel operated. I didn't fault Mom. How would she know any different? And Brittany helped as much as possible. But neither of them had the education or experience to successfully run this place. Or heck, even just to keep it afloat. If I could make heads or tails about the books, I might be able to convince a buyer to take over. It was such a bummer it had gone downhill.

I tapped my pen against the thick book. "Mom, let's see if we can get the most recent books organized today. Let's focus on just the previous month." I'd give her the fact she tracked items in the log, but any sort of system? Not even close. "Brittany, I'm thinking if we had a white board in here, we could use that as we work through each item. Left column expenses, right column revenue. Would you be able to go the office supply story in Emerald Hills and pick that up?"

"Sure, Aunt Chloe. Anything else?"

"Do you have cleaning supplies here? I want it to look as nice as possible when guests come. We need repeat business and some good reviews to boost the desirability."

"Chloe, it gives it a rustic charm." Mom sat in the corner, flipping through her magazine. "You know in the olden days they didn't have maids like you had at your house. You shouldn't criticize it. We get a lot of compliments on how authentic the place is."

I seriously doubted that. But a dust rag once in a while wouldn't hurt. I looked over at the dogs and saw Trixie's white coat looking more like charcoal and chestnut with no hint of white. Max had cleared out a spot on the floor and his nose was covered in dust bunnies. I took a deep breath to gather my thoughts. It was easy to criticize. I'd work on building Mom up. I didn't know how much more time we had together, and I needed to make the most of it.

"More coffee, Brittany," I said. "I'm afraid to plug in that coffee maker."

Brittany stood. "Yeah, we've had smoke coming out of it from time to time."

"Would you want to take the pups with you for a road trip? I think they're going to get antsy staying here for too long."

"Sure, c'mon, guys. Let's go on a ride." Brittany waved them through the door.

Trixie leapt up and body-checked Max. He paused, letting her take the lead. I worried Trixie's assertive ways would further push Max into his shell. I'd need to keep an eye on her to make sure she didn't bully him. He was my number one. When that bossy little girl entered the picture, he probably wondered who was this thing rocking his world?

"OK, Mom. While we're waiting for Brittany to get our supplies, let's start organizing these binders." I pushed all of the tables into a row so we could line up the books in what I hoped was some semblance of chronological order. There was one small window to the side of the room. It did little to lighten the place. I moved a lamp closer to our work area, which didn't provide much more light beyond what you might see in a rustic cabin with no electricity. I should have added a lamp to Brittany's shopping list. Or ten lamps. Onward. Mom and I lugged six of the binders to the table. I opened the first one, and dust flew.

"Mom, do you have any blank or unused books? I think I might have to start fresh with some of these."

"Of course, Chloe. I'm not totally incompetent." She brought two large notebooks to the table and dropped them next to me. Another cloud of dust rose up. When she came in, Brittany would be hard-pressed to see us, cloaked in this shroud. I sure hoped the pups didn't have an issue with the dust.

"Mom, it looks like this binder starts with January of this year. Let's go through that. Maybe the more recent ones will be easier to remember."

Mom shrugged. "Whatever you say, Chloe. You're the expert."

"We need this as orderly as possible to attract a buyer."

"Oh, Chloe. I can't sell. This is Marty's legacy. He'd roll over in his grave. I just need you to get it organized and then I can take it from there. I'm sure you'll do better than that incompetent accountant. I wish I'd never hired him. Even I could tell he was a dunce with the numbers."

I hoped I could live up to her expectations. The place had so much potential. Back in the day, it was booked solid, a real destination hotel. It had become a kind of community hub with fun events and outdoor adventures year-round.

"We'll just need to make a best guess for what's in the books." I sat in the chair with the book on my lap. "Let's see if we can get through one book a day." At least that was a start to piece together this puzzle. "January second, Pete's Plumbing. OK. That's a great start. Do you remember where you had plumbing work done?" Max's eyebrows twitched as if I was on the right path.

"Of course. It was that persnickety Snowberry Sanctuary. Having a hot tub in that unit is such a pain. There's always one problem or another with it."

The Snowberry Sanctuary was our highest-end rental. It was the largest at nine hundred square feet. The territorial view felt like you were on top of the world. If you didn't know better, you'd think you were in a four-star hotel room. It was also the place that required the most work and was rented the least of any of the treehouses. After getting these books together, we needed to seriously consider decommissioning that unit. Or at least simplifying it for maintenance purposes.

"What's this second entry? It just says 'Joey' for five hundred dollars."

"Your sister always needs money for rent or bailing someone out of jail. You know, she doesn't make very much working at that restaurant. And at her age, she shouldn't be a waitress. But what else can she do?"

"Mom, you can't use the business money for personal use. Is it just this one time or is there more?"

Mom waved her hand in the air. "You know Joey. She's always got some emergency or another."

"I'm going to get a second notebook to write down personal expenses. Can we agree from now on you don't pay personal items from the business account?"

"You're the expert," she said for the second time. "I'll do what you say. I wish Joey was more like you. Then I wouldn't have to keep rescuing her. I'm so glad you're here." Mom reached across the table for my hand. "I mean, with you helping solve Edna's death. I'm sure you'll be able to figure it out. You're really good at those number puzzles. What are they?"

"Sudoku." I was pretty good, regularly solving at least the hard level. If you worked it enough, you eventually figured it out. There was always an answer, you just had to be persistent and try different options. Max and I teamed up on those, sometimes setting a timer to see how fast we could get the answers.

"Plus, you were married to a cop. So you probably picked up a lot from that about detective work."

"Mom, let's just keep to the task at hand." I flipped through a few more books, skimming. "Reconstructing these books is going to take

37

all of my time and energy. I told you I'm only here for six months to help you through this so the hotel can be listed for sale. I have my own life away from here."

Mom sighed. "I know. But it would be so nice to have my family together again. We could really use you here to help with Joey. She has all those kids and grandkids. I can't even keep track there's so many now. We'd only need Harrison to move back so we could all be like it was before. I mean, how could my only son leave his mom like that?" Harrison had followed my path and beat feet out of town as soon as he'd finished school.

"Let's keep going on the books." The next couple of entries looked pretty straightforward. Thank heaven for that. *Good job, Mom.*

"Chloe, doesn't that sound nice? We were such a happy family when we were all together. I want that again before I die. I don't know how much more time I have."

Oh boy. Guilt trip commenced. Buckle up for a ride down the well-worn path. Mom tried hard, but her choices fell short. She always felt as if she should have a husband. Mostly, for someone to help with the kids. But who wants a ready-made family? That's a big reason I have Max. He knows what I'm thinking and totally gets me. When I need a pick-me-up, he grins as wide as a Muppet and wags his stubby little tail to make me grin. It works every time.

CHAPTER SIX

B uzz had a good thing going with his barber shop. The exterior had a quaint, inviting look with the classic barber pole and a large, square window that took up most of the front wall bordering the sidewalk. He had a little flag posted out front, reading *Now Open*. The door was propped open to let in a lovely, cool breeze. Buzz had a recliner brought in to use when he wasn't working. His feet propped up with a newspaper draped across his midsection.

"Hi, Buzz."

He twitched, faking as if I didn't wake him from a slumber.

"Hey, Chloe. C'mon in." He lowered the footrest of the recliner, crumpled the paper, and plopped it onto a side table. "I was just catching up on the news."

It boggled my mind how this town managed to keep a local newspaper going.

"Thanks. I'm just checking in on any progress in Edna's death. You know I'm not going to get a moment's peace at home until this is solved. And frankly, I need all the energy I have to keep going through the books at the hotel."

"Yeah, that's gotta be somethin'. I hope you get it sorted out."

"Maybe you could come help? I sure could use your detective skills. It's a real head-scratcher for most of what I'm finding."

Buzz chuckled, his belly jiggling up and down.

"Well, this thing with Edna is about all I can do. There's a reason I retired from the force and took up snipping hair. I don't usually have to haul people off to jail at the end of the appointment." He laughed at his own joke. His middle jiggled again.

I took a seat in the only guest chair in the place.

"You know it. Perks of retirement. That men's club, though. More drama than a high school play. But that's a story for another day. You'll have to dust off your clubs and play a round while you're still here."

"Brilliant idea. I need to get out of the house and that dingy hotel. I have a sinking feeling that even after all the time I spend getting the books in order, we won't be able to find a buyer. If only Mom considered selling when it was still doing well."

"So I talked with the boys in Emerald Hills. They've got to be the ones to handle this."

"Any update yet on cause of death? Edna wasn't a young chick. But Mom has her suspicions of something nefarious. You know how it is once the gossip train leaves the station and gains some steam."

"Pretty much. There's no stopping it. You just have to wait until a new topic comes up and then it's off to the races again. It's so nice having you back, Chloe. Even if it's just for a short time."

Buzz was a good guy. I thought so in high school and he'd maintained that 'til now. We'd dated for a year before I left. We had really enjoyed our time together, but it was clear we'd never be more than just friends. I'd left on good terms. "Yeah, you know why I can't stay."

"I know. But maybe there's a way you can come back and maintain your own identity. Your independence from your family. You shouldn't have to feel compelled to rescue them anymore. And Harrison isn't even in town." Buzz had been my confidant in those years before I moved away. He knew the nitty-gritty of what I'd had to do to manage the household when Mom wasn't there.

"I'll think about it. But I don't see it happening. So what's the verdict from the Emerald Hills guys? What do they have so far?"

"Can we keep this between us for now?" Buzz's tone was ominous.

"Um, OK. You've got me worried, Buzz."

"Well, there's several things that appear questionable. Until they can rule them out, we don't need to fuel the fire."

"Like what?" I got up and stood against the wall.

"Right now, they're looking into how she got a bump on her head."

I gasped. "Buzz, what are they thinking?"

"Chloe, one step at a time. It could be anything. She could have tripped and hit her head on something. You know how that little Trixie of hers was always underfoot."

"Indeed. That girl is clingy. And she's quite the pest to Max. What else?" I paced, wondering how I'd keep a straight face when I got home. I needed a cover story to hold off Mom's grilling.

"Those morning glory vines were everywhere. She may have tripped on those. That gazing globe was off its stand, in pieces. Really, Chloe, we could speculate all day long. We've got to establish some facts and data before we get too far."

"The Garden Club yesterday had this wild idea." I thought Buzz was going to lose it.

He doubled over and slapped his knee.

"That's a statement of the obvious. Do tell. What's the latest from the ladies?"

I didn't want to say. It was pretty far-fetched. But you had to rule things out too. "They think she ate some poisonous flowers by mistake." There. The cockamamie idea was now out there.

Buzz was silent. He rubbed his chin. He looked at me, then got out of the chair, went to the mini-fridge, and got a bottle of beer. He snapped off the top and handed it to me. I was tempted but shook my head. He took a long swig, draining about half the bottle. He wiped his mouth with his hand and returned to the chair.

"Chloe, I'm trying to discount that for every reason I can think of. But that might not be as crazy as it sounds. On the one hand, she was a master gardener, winning all of those awards. On the other hand, she did make all of those dishes with edible flowers. Could she have inadvertently mixed them up?"

"I don't want to make this worse, Buzz. But I think we should be looking at everything."

"*We?* Now I have a partner?"

"Well, Mom's more upset than she's letting on. I need this resolved for her. I'll do what I can. I mean, I did learn a thing or two from Frank during all those years he was on the force."

Buzz frowned. "Patience, Chloe. Let's get that round of golf on the books. See what you got after all these years."

"Sounds good, Buzz. It's great to catch up with you. I better scoot. Gotta make sure the house is still in one piece. I'm more worried about Mom than the dogs. And I need some rest for another day excavating those hotel books."

Buzz got up and we hugged. I was thankful for this calm, bright spot in my day. I was headed back to the hotel to see what mayhem had ensued with my absence.

CHAPTER SEVEN

Trixie busted through the door first, seemingly more energy than when she left. Max trailed behind with Brittany to avoid getting in Trixie's line of fire. She wiggled her body all the way across the room for a greeting from Mom, who ignored her. She made some sort of low gurgle noise to get attention and retreated a step, still wiggling beyond belief. No acknowledgment from Mom brought a higher-pitched rumble from her and another step back. She continued this until she was at a total ear-piercing bark.

Mom cracked a smile and relented.

"OK, girl. I hear you." She scratched Trixie behind the ears with both hands. Serenity for a moment. Trixie moved on to me, like we were the royal receiving party. I quickly gave her the ear scratch as well.

Brittany made eye contact with me to assess the situation. I shrugged a bit. "Thank you so much for getting our supplies. Especially the java." I retrieved the carrier with three beverages, and she returned to her car for the remaining items. "Mom, let's take a break and have some coffee. I can only look at those for so long before my brain starts to fog up."

"It's not that bad, Chloe. You could stand to be more positive and not complain so much." I bit my tongue. Maybe she was right.

Brittany returned. "Aunt Chloe, where do you want these? I got three of them." She lugged the first whiteboard inside.

I moved a table closer to the wall and propped it up so we could all see it. Brittany left the room to retrieve the remaining items. I wasn't sure using these would help much, but it would allow us to better organize the materials and maybe speed up the process. A small puff of dust rose from an overstuffed chair as Mom retrieved her coffee and took a seat. The chair faced away from our work area, as if Mom was in time out.

"Brittany, thank you so much for running the errand. I hope having the pups with you wasn't too much trouble."

Trixie settled on the fleece throw that I had when I first adopted Max. Like everything of his, she'd claimed it as her own in a matter of a day.

Max, the gentleman, stood next to her pondering his next move. He acquiesced and plopped onto the floor, one paw on the blanket. A message of peace but not full surrender. My sweet, sweet boy. *I'm sorry she's totally turned your life upside down. It's just for now, boy. I'll figure something out soon.*

"Nah, they were great," Brittany said. "I put both of them in the back, but Trixie insisted she be in the front seat. I think that was better for Max too. She kept pushing him to the side so she could see out the front."

Max looked at me to confirm the account. Brittany patted him on the head. Trixie bolted up, intervened, and almost toppled Max. He stumbled, and seeing his opportunity, tiptoed around her to take a seat on the blanket. Oblivious, Trixie usurped Brittany's attention.

"Well, thanks again, Britt. We're taking a coffee break, then back at it. I set this up to try and have a system to go through the books from this year as a start."

Trixie turned and spotted Max on the blanket. She stood right next to him and flung her body practically on top of him. He raised his head and pleaded for help. He couldn't have looked less comfortable but wouldn't yield an inch. I'd have to be more thoughtful about each of them having enough of everything.

"Oh, smart, Aunt Chloe. That'll make it easier to remember some of the stuff. I'll help however I can."

Mom sipped her coffee, giving me the silent treatment. I really did need to find a way to get along with her.

"Chloe, why don't we do a big family dinner?" she asked, coming back to the conversation. "I would love to have my daughters back together again."

I looked at Brittany and paused before my reply. *Be the bigger person, Chloe.* "OK, Mom. I'll have to figure out when I have time."

"Chloe, you make time for family." She rose from the chair and returned to the work area. "Oh, this will be great. You girls back together. Too bad Harrison moved away. You know, he hardly ever calls me."

My baby brother had the same idea when he graduated from high school. He didn't have a destination, but instead packed up his car with everything he had and just started driving east. Maybe I'd reach out to him again and let him know what was going on with Mom. He might want one last chance to mend the relationship. No matter what happened, she was our mom.

"Sounds good, Mom."

"Fabulous! I'll start the planning." She got a notebook and started jotting ideas down.

I took a sip of my coffee. "Mom, we've got a lot of work to do here. I need you to help."

"Oh, Brittany can do that. She knows as much as I do about what's going on."

I looked at Brittany. She gave a small nod yes. That was probably just as well. I wondered if all this was for naught, or would I be successful in my mission?

CHAPTER EIGHT

Brittany and I had finished our coffee. "OK, Britt. Let's see if we can get through January and February by lunch time. It's a lot. But if we don't get hung up on every minuscule detail, I think we can do it."

"Sure thing."

Max came over and assumed the position he always held when we solved our puzzles. He raised his paw and placed it at my elbow. He rested his snout on the book to help me with the clues. "We just started January and got through about the first week." I turned the page of the notebook and dust flew. I scratched my nose and rubbed my eyes. This place could use a good vacuum.

We worked through week two of January. Brittany did have a better memory recall, so this went more smoothly. Some legit expenses, some of Mom's shenanigans. *That's OK. It's a starting point to improve upon.*

"Great job, Brittany. Let's do week three." We started to get into a rhythm. The more recent entries were a piece of cake. I was petrified of finishing this and going back to prior years. I'd save that for later. Maybe we could get away with not doing that for now. I opened another book and more dust emerged. Max sneezed and shook his head to clear it out. Trixie glared at the nerve of him to disturb her peace. He looked at me and gave a big grin.

A loud ring startled the dogs so much that Trixie jumped up and yelped. Her face looked perplexed like she wondered who dared disturb the princess with that obnoxious noise. Max stood and watched the Trixie show. Danger, schmanger.

Mom hadn't replaced the office phone yet with a cell phone. It rang the old-fashioned ring. I felt like I'd need to ask Ernestine to patch me through. I reached the source of Trixie's annoyance and answered the phone. She ceased barking. "Cedarbrook Treehouse Hotel. Chloe speaking. How can I help you?"

Mom's nose was still buried in the family reunion planning notebook, oblivious to a customer calling.

"Hi, Arthur. What can I do for you?"

Mom looked inquisitively at me. I shrugged my shoulders. It was a short conversation, and when I finished, I hung up the phone.

"Edna had a nephew?" I had no idea. But I'd been gone so long I wasn't in the know.

"Not that I know of," Mom said.

"Me neither," Brittany said.

"Well that guy, Arthur, said he was her nephew. He lives in Oklahoma. He called over to Edna's and whoever answered the phone told him to call me and tell him what happened. Not sure how I landed smack dab in the middle of this." The more I tried to keep arm's length of anything going on in this town, the more I got sucked in. It was a vortex of histrionics with no escape.

"What did he want?" Mom asked.

"Not exactly sure. Except he quizzed me about where Edna's stuff would end up. He didn't even express any sympathy or ask about a service for her." What was his angle? I wasn't aware of any relatives who might inherit her estate. Her boyfriend Ralph wouldn't be the one since they'd never married.

"So, Chloe. We'll have to drive out to Zoe's to invite her to the family dinner. I think she lives so far away without a phone so she doesn't have to call or see me. And Joey works at the restaurant, so that's an easy one. I don't think she'll ever leave that place. I mean, what else could she do? She never went to college like you did, Chloe."

Oh, Mom. "Well, we have a lot to do here. So it won't be anytime soon." I needed to focus on getting these books in order. Second, spending time fixing it up could prove fruitful. I had some rookie knowledge of repairs from the projects Frank and I had completed. "Mom, what do you think about sprucing up around here? I think we could do some things to make it look pretty good. I might as well take advantage of my time here. I've got some ideas for decorating and getting the grounds shaped up."

"That sounds great, Chloe. Maybe I could bring some of my garden gnomes to cheer it up." Hmm. Maybe. Max looked up at me and questioned that suggestion too. Those little creatures probably wigged him out as much as they did me. He was eye level with them. Maybe we could put them in their own little section.

Brittany and I resumed our rhythm of review. We'd gotten through January and were into February. Thankfully, there were a few patterns I spotted and some repeated entries, making it a bit easier to decipher. Why did Arthur's phone call bother me? I couldn't put a finger on it. I'd met selfish people all my life. Maybe he was in shock. Since I didn't know him, maybe he didn't come across as caring in general. Nope, not that. I did not have a good feeling about him.

CHAPTER NINE

"Good morning, Mom." Trixie and Max had already been up, outside for play, had breakfast, and were lounging next to me on the patio. With that rest, they were eager for another playmate. But it wouldn't be Mom. They took off on a race around the yard.

"Chloe, can you keep those dogs quiet?" Mom shuffled her slippered feet through the patio door to the kitchen. "I just got up and I haven't even had coffee yet. Look what they're doing, knocking things over."

I needed to corral them or we'd have an incident on our hands. I noticed one of Mom's cherished gnomes in her set of *See No Evil, Hear No Evil, Speak No Evil* had been knocked over. I'd have to set it back up or she'd have a fit.

"Max. Trixie. Time to go inside." They stopped in their tracks and pleaded for more romp time. "Sorry guys, we'll play more later." They followed me inside. Trixie, of course, had taken over Max's larger bed. Only the best for the princess. Max had squeezed his body into Trixie's smaller bed, looking like Goldilocks in Baby Bear's bed. Good enough for now. I couldn't have my sensitive boy's feelings hurt. He would always be my number one.

Mom ambled back into the dining room, her hair a bird's nest, her light pink fluffy robe cinched tight around her waist. She'd had that ratty thing as long as I could remember. She plopped into the seat across from me and let out a noisy sigh. I didn't bite.

"Mom, Buzz and I are heading to Edna's this morning for a bit. We're going to meet Detective Jansen from Emerald Hills to look over things. It appears Edna's death is suspicious."

Mom perked up as if she'd had three cups of coffee. "Oooo, Chloe. I knew it. Call me right after that. I have to know what happens."

Uh, no. She could wait until I got home. One word to her and the town crier would have the news blasted before I even returned.

"I doubt I'll know anything more. I'm heading out in a bit. I'm going to take just Max this time and give him a break from Trixie. Then, I'll be back to get you and head to the hotel."

"That's fine. She's not too bad when she's by herself."

I think she secretly liked the company. Last night before bed, Trixie had snuggled up next to Mom on the couch, and they looked like they'd been made for each other.

———ele———

I pulled up to Edna's house within a few minutes of leaving home. The detective's car was parked parallel to the house. Buzz's car was in the driveway. Thankfully, we'd have a chance to talk details without being interrupted. I parked behind the detective's car and headed into the house. My stomach was unsure if it was upset over the breakfast I ate or the thought of entering a deceased person's home. I opened the screen door and entered. The old lady smell was just as it was the day we found Edna. I followed the sound of voices to the garden. Buzz and the detective stood just outside the sliding door.

"Hi, Chloe," Buzz said. "We waited for you. This is Detective Jansen from the Emerald Hill's office.

Rudy, this is Chloe. One of my dear friends from yesteryear." Buzz and his belly jiggled at the funny. Rudy and I shook hands. He was taller than Buzz, but most everyone was. His hair had thinned on top and the sides grayed just a touch. Distinguished, as they say about men when their aging shows.

"Nice to meet you. Not sure how I can help. Where's Ralph? I saw the Studebaker, but his other car's gone."

"He let us in, then went to do some errands. I think it's all still too fresh for him."

"We're just surveying the scene right now. The preliminary autopsy report indicated a large contusion on the right rear of her head. We're trying to piece together a scenario that could explain that. She was face down. If she'd fallen and then hit her head, the contusion would likely be on the front, or even the side. But not the back. Let's go to where she fell and see what the view looks like from there."

Edna's garden was magazine-worthy. She manicured every bush, tree, and flower for a picture-perfect scene. The winding brick paths led around bird baths, waterfalls, and several garden gnomes. I didn't know what people saw in those odd little creatures. Both her and Mom had taken up collecting the kooky ceramics. It had become a competition between the two as to who had the better collection. Edna had the same set as Mom. Although her *Speak No Evil* was missing. Max had wandered off the path to the set, noticing the absence of the third gnome. The fact it was gone, an oddity. We wound our way through to the location where Edna's body had been found.

"So I'm going to stand in the spot where Edna's feet were when she fell," the detective said. "Let's see what that perspective brings for any further explanation." Buzz and I remained a few steps back. "OK, from here I can see the stand where the gazing globe had been. But it's nowhere near her, so I don't see how she could have fallen onto it."

We stood there, soaking in the picture, willing it to speak some answers.

"Those morning glory vines are covering part of the walkway. Could she have tripped on those?" Buzz asked.

"Possibly," Detective Jansen said. "We've got a couple of key questions to answer. That's one of them. The other is how did she get the contusion?"

"Her dog could also have made her stumble. She's small and gets underfoot at times," I said.

"Possibly." He pressed his lips into a thin line.

He kept things close to the vest. They probably teach you that in detective school. Never share details with a civilian.

"I'm going to make some drawings before I go," the detective continued. "Sometimes, letting these things percolate can help guide you to the answers." He took out a sketchpad and pencil and started drawing. He walked ten feet to the right side where Edna's head had faced, turned around and drew some more. He continued viewing the scene from all angles to complete his picture. "Thank you both for your help. I'll be in touch."

I was actually thankful he hadn't shared much. That way I could truthfully tell Mom I didn't know. We silently retraced our steps through the garden and house to the driveway. We all shook hands and said we'd look forward to an update. I got in my car and headed home to gather Mom.

Max looked at me and whimpered. "I know, boy. This is our biggest puzzle yet to solve. Good job noticing that gnome was missing." Who could possibly want to hurt Edna? Frank was suspiciously absent at just the right time. And Caroline found her. Was the Garden Club presidency that big of a deal to her reputation?

CHAPTER TEN

M om, the pups, and I had eaten lunch at home and been at the office about an hour. We were getting into a rhythm of reviewing her books and deciphering the entries. Our success rate was about 50 percent, guessing the entry correctly or giving up and putting it into a *we gave it our best shot* bucket.

"So, Chloe. When we go visit Zoe later, don't be shocked by what you see. I mean she's living the hippie lifestyle, not a care in the world."

"Thanks for the heads-up, Mom." I had no idea what to expect. Zoe lived with her boyfriend of many years, off-grid. In a way, that sounded wonderful. That type of living fit my criteria for being independent and having my own identity.

"I mean, she doesn't even have a phone to call her. How backwoods is that? Even I'm up with the times and have a cell phone." She was so not up with the times. Case in point: the hotel bookkeeping.

I looked forward to seeing Zoe. The previous times I had visited Cedarbrook it was a crap shoot whether I'd see her or not. She kept to herself but was friendly when we got together. I'd never been to her place. We'd always met at Mom's, and that never gave us much of a chance to talk freely.

Mom licked her thumb and flipped a page of the book in front of her. "It's going to be so great when we all get together for our dinner."

It was going to be something. Great was a stretch. I'd take civil.

"I'm looking forward to it. I wanted to make sure to see Zoe and Joey before I leave." I kept reiterating my plans to keep them on Mom's radar. She talked as if I had come back for good. Not even close. Six months was a huge commitment to stay and help prepare the hotel for sale. The main thing keeping my sanity was knowing there was an end date to my term.

"Chloe, I just know after our dinner you'll want to stay. It will be great to have my daughters together again before I die. I'll be so happy."

The door to the office opened, letting in much needed light. If I stayed in town, and Mom retained the hotel, there was a growing list of upgrades I wanted to make. A new window or two in the office was one of them. I looked up, fully expecting to see Brittany. I did a double take since the person had long brown hair like my niece. The individual entering, however, was taller and a little heavier than Britt. He held the door open, as if pondering his decision to fully enter the room.

"Can I help you?" I asked.

"Yes, I'd like to rent one of your treehouses, if you have one available."

I sat stunned, not sure if I'd heard correctly. We actually had a customer.

"I'm sorry?" I said, wanting to confirm what I understood.

"Do you not have any available?"

"Oh no, we do." I scrambled to meet him at the desk we used for checking in. Mom followed. She stood behind me with her arms folded as she assessed the young man, with his long hair, baggy jeans, and sloppy plaid shirt. "We have a few choices of cabins for you. Do you have any specific requests?"

"We need a deposit first," Mom blurted.

I closed my eyes for a second.

"What she means is that we'll need a credit card for the reservation. But we won't charge you until you leave."

"That's not what I mean," Mom continued. "We can't have people coming in, thinking they can stiff us. So we need to be paid up front."

Wow! No wonder the place felt like a ghost town; she had the most unwelcoming attitude.

"It's OK." He shrugged. "I have cash."

Max nonchalantly strolled over and stood right next to me. He was so close I felt a low rumble from his body. He looked up at me to affirm his displeasure with this guest. *I know, boy. Something doesn't seem right with me either.*

I opened the reservation book and handed him a card to fill out. "Great. Let's get you registered, then I'll take you to the Huckleberry Hut." As long as I was here, we'd have great customer service. Huckleberry Hut was one of our more basic units. The size resembled a standard hotel room. It was also currently the cleanest, bedding laundered and room dusted, waiting for a guest.

Mom hadn't budged, her arms wrapped tight around her in skepticism.

"That sounds nice," the man said.

Huckleberry Hut was one of the few cabins with most everything working. The heater was kaput. But since the weather was warmer that wasn't an immediate issue. I just hoped he thought it was nice when he actually saw the place. He filled out the registration card and I took his money for the first night.

"How long will you be staying with us?" I asked.

"Not sure. Just needed a getaway from the rat race for a few days." I nodded. "What do you recommend for a restaurant?"

"There's not much in town. Nothing you'd like." Mom couldn't have tried harder to deter him from staying.

Well, this explained why the hotel wasn't profitable. "There's the Smokehouse Restaurant for a nice sit down meal. And a little deli or a burger place for to-go items."

"You probably won't like them." Mom continued her rant.

We were saved by the interruption of Brittany arriving in the office. Thankfully she'd been visiting each cabin to make sure they weren't in total disarray from critters or some such thing.

"Hi Britt. Would you please take our new guest to the Huckleberry Hut?" I grabbed the dusty key from the wall hook, nonchalantly wiping the grime from it before handing it to Brittany.

"Sure thing. Right this way."

The door closed and I wheeled around. "You could be nicer to the guests. They're the only glimmer we have of keeping this place afloat to attract a decent buyer." Max walked over to Mom, tilted his head, and arched an eyebrow. He seemed to be taking her side.

"He's going to stiff us. I can tell his type. If you had more experience here, Chloe, you'd be able to tell that too." She returned to her chair at our worktable.

"What's his *type*, Mom? Paying customer?" I couldn't help myself. My mouth and my brain were not in sync. I inhaled through my chest and diaphragm, holding my breath for five seconds and slowly letting it out.

"Mark my words, Chloe. A sloppy guy dressed like your hippie sister is bad news. I've been doing this long enough that I've seen it all. And he smelled like the pot. We don't need druggies here."

A little part of me wondered that too. But no chance I'd give her the satisfaction of agreeing before it actually happened. I'd wait and see. Hope for the best.

"When Brittany gets back to hold down the fort, let's head out to Zoe's." My strategy to change the subject when Mom went down a rathole with her negative comments usually worked. I looked at the calendar and counted the number of days until I returned home. My own home.

"You're right." Mom stood. "We should go soon. It's so far out in the boonies it takes forever to get there. I'll never know why they felt the need to build a house a million miles away."

I left it at that.

CHAPTER ELEVEN

Mom was right about the boonies. I was pretty sure we'd been in the car an hour and hadn't seen a house in a while. Talk about separation. Thankfully, I'd looked at the GPS ahead of time and an overhead map. That gave me a general sense of direction we were headed. The thick forest made everything look identical. Passing mile marker thirty-two was the landmark I was looking for. A lightly graveled, mostly dirt road led into the grove of trees. We began our trek down the pothole lined route for who knows how long. The gullies were so deep the dogs bounced in the back seat like they were on a trampoline. Walking from here might have been a better plan, but I had no idea how much farther we had to go. I slowed as much as I could but still kept the momentum.

"You were right, Mom. This couldn't be more secluded if they tried."

"You always were the most responsible and logical one. If only you'd stayed in town, maybe Zoe and Joey could have had your positive influence. When you were taking care of things at home, everything was so much better."

We continued bounding down the path, Mom's small stature a benefit so she didn't carom off the roof as we descended some of the holes.

She gazed out the window, in her own reality. "At least we always had a roof over our heads, and food and clothes." She sniffled. Her voice cracked.

"I'm just glad that somehow you found Marty. He was such a gem. His kindness was all that you deserve, Mom." She extracted a tissue from her purse and blew her nose. "Do you know about how much longer before we're there?"

"How do I know, Chloe?"

The pups had settled into the seat, figuring that if they hugged it they'd be better than ricocheting off the ceiling. Max was off to the side, Trixie hogging the middle view. I couldn't wait to reward them with a romp around the place when we arrived. I'm sure they could use the stress relief too. We must have traveled for at least another ten minutes before the sky lightened above. Max stood and caught my eye in the rear-view mirror. He grinned wide. I couldn't resist that smooshy face, ever. I matched his smile, my spirits instantly perked. His tail wiggled in response.

"Mom, I'm sorry about Edna. I know you two had your moments in the past. But I see that her death is hitting you hard."

She continued her gaze out the window.

"I'm surprised about it, myself," Mom said. "She was such a snot most of the time when I was married to Lloyd. She was a spoiled-rotten daddy's girl. Got everything she wanted. She could do no wrong in Lloyd's eyes. I think that was one of the reasons we got divorced."

"That must have been a sad time for you." All of her kids were out of the house when she'd married Lloyd. I'm sure the empty nest feeling contributed to her loneliness. From four kids in the zoo to zero kids and deathly quiet. I know after Frank passed, the quiet ate away at my brain. My mind aimlessly wandered to some not so happy places. Mom had always lived with another person, and when Lloyd left it probably broke her heart. I needed to find some answers about Edna so Mom had some peace.

"Yeah, it was. I always wondered if I could have done something differently. I tried to get along with Edna, but she created wedges between Lloyd and me on a regular basis. I think to spite me, she kept that beautiful antique ring he promised to me. She'd wear it around and flaunt it. I guess to prove to herself that she won the love competition of her father."

This was probably the most vulnerable my mom had ever been with me. For the remainder of my time in town, I'd prioritize encouraging. Everyone deserved happiness.

"It looks like we might be there." I hit the last pothole and launched into a wide open space. I saw the cutest little log house and what must have been a barn. At least ten sheep inhabited a corral. I spotted pigs and chickens and a vegetable garden that could have fed an army. I have to say, it wasn't what I expected. I pulled up to the house entryway and parked. Trixie let loose with a thundering yip like she was escaping a long stint in prison. She scrambled to the front seat and squirted out my door as I opened it. Max looked at me, requesting permission. He had better manners than most people I knew. I nodded and he followed Trixie's path to freedom. I circled the car to help Mom out. I reached my hand to support her exit and she waved it off.

"I can do it, Chloe. I'm not a cripple, you know." I withdrew my hand and held the door. She hoisted herself out, steadied on her feet, and marched off toward the front door. The dogs, enamored with the animals, watched the other creatures as if at a zoo.

Zoe emerged from the house as we approached. "Hello," she greeted. *Let the games begin.*

CHAPTER TWELVE

Her smile as wide as the open space on the property, Zoe had aged beautifully. Her long, flowing silver hair cascaded behind her. Her arms were outstretched for a warm hug, her multi-colored three-fourths length skirt a testament to her wild side.

"Hi, Chloe. You look amazing. Retirement agrees with you." My sister embraced me long and hard. She released and continued to hold my hand. Looking deeply into my eyes, she said, "I was so sorry to hear about Frank."

"Thank you."

"Can we go inside?" Mom wrinkled her nose. "It stinks out here."

"Of course, Mom. I made some raspberry scones to go with our tea." Zoe squeezed my hand and led the way into the house.

"Max, Trixie." They stopped in their tracks, incredulous I'd interrupt nirvana. Reluctantly, my boy obeyed. Begrudgingly, Trixie followed. They followed Zoe inside and collapsed on the floor, panting, tongues extended.

It was a beautiful log cabin that Zoe and her boyfriend had milled out of logs from their own property. The surrounding landscape had natural growth that showed loving care. What they had built for themselves was impressive and quite an accomplishment. I would love to use their expertise to enhance the hotel. With their eye to beautify using nature, they could do wonders for making it more attractive.

The inside of the house was just as comfortable, a sanctuary in itself. The furniture was also built from wood on their property. We entered the kitchen and sat at the table. A platter filled with scones sat center place. A teapot on the stove began to warm for our accompanying beverages.

"It still smells like a pig sty in here. I don't know how you stand it, Zoe. I don't think I can eat with that smell. It's making me nauseous."

Zoe angled away from Mom toward me. "So Chloe, tell me how things are going with the hotel."

"We're making good progress going through the books. I'm hopeful we can get those in shape and then get a realtor to list it for sale. My goal is to be back home before winter."

"Chloe, you know I don't want to sell the place." Mom crossed her arms. "I just needed your help to get it up and running in good shape again. Then I can take it back over. Zoe, can you talk some sense into her moving back home? I still never understood why you girls moved so far away from home." Mom scoffed. "Can I just get a glass of water?"

Zoe rose from the table and went to the refrigerator to get a pitcher of filtered water. She poured a glass of crystal clear liquid. She set it in front of Mom who raised it up and examined it like a specimen. "Is this from your water barrel?"

"Yes, Mom. It's from our rain catchment system. It's perfectly fine to drink. We filter it so the taste is actually very good."

Mom set the glass down in front of her. "No thanks."

I put one of the scones on a serving plate as Zoe prepared our tea. "Mom, do you want tea? The water is boiled, further removing the impurities."

She raised her nose in the air. "I guess that would be OK. I need to use the restroom. That drive is so long out here. Do you still have that outhouse toilet?"

"It's a composting toilet, Mom. And yes, we still have that. Just do your business and I'll take care of the rest."

Mom harrumphed off to the bathroom. When she was out of earshot, Zoe said, "Chloe, you're a saint for coming to help her with the hotel. I'm really hoping she sells that place. It's too much for her and there's no way she can run it on her own. But then what would she do with her time?"

"Well," I said, "probably more of what she does now. Gossip and garage sales. Her collection of garden gnomes is insane. It's taken over her yard and moved into the house. And I find it especially creepy. But to each his own."

Zoe sat down at the table. "Chloe, are you really leaving after the hotel is listed for sale?"

"I have to, Zoe. You understand why."

"I know how it was all of those years ago. Some things are the same, but not everything. If you moved back, you could have the relationship with Mom on your terms. Be clear about your boundaries and hold to them. No guilt, no shame. I'd sure love to see you more often too. Heck, you could even come stay with us however long you needed for a break. You know Max would relish living the life of a sheepdog." Right on cue, Max sauntered over, his tongue lolled out of his mouth, taking Zoe's side.

"See? He's totally on board."

I imagined the thought of staying here, just my boy and me. Zoe could sweet talk with the best of them. She made a good case, lots of merits.

"I don't know, Zoe. It'd be such a big change for me after all this time."

"Just think about it, OK?"

I consented so that we ended this conversation before Mom returned to the room. I loved the allure of the nature and privacy.

"Zoe, why can't you live like a normal person? I mean, this backwoods stuff is ridiculous. You can't even have a proper hairdo. Look at Chloe's beautiful hair. It's nice and neat even though it's fake blonde. With all of the money I gave you, I'd think you would have a better house and better clothes."

Mom tapped the side of her teacup. "Chloe, tell your sister how you're helping solve Edna's murder."

"Mom, we don't know how she died yet. It could have been an accident." If I let on about my suspicions of murder, I wouldn't be able to get that genie back in the bottle.

"You know, she was always arguing with Ralph. It was either money or her jealousy about his prior relationship with Caroline. I think he had something to do with it, just to shut her up." Mom's theories just kept on coming. "Zoe, we're having a family dinner so you have to come."

"Of course, Mom. Just let me know when and what I can bring. We'll be there."

"Well, Eldon doesn't have to come. This is just for family." Until Zoe and Eldon married, Mom would never consider him part of the family, and likely never would. I think she blamed him for taking Zoe away from her.

I stood. "We should get going. We've got a long drive back and I'm going to check on Ralph later today to see how he's doing. Even if they fought a lot, he's still grieving." Mom grabbed her purse and beelined for the door like the place was on fire.

"Great," she said over her shoulder. "Grill him good. And let me know what he says. I never liked him, anyway."

CHAPTER THIRTEEN

I pulled into the driveway at Ralph and Edna's house. I felt bad that Ralph didn't have much help to take care of Edna's affairs, so I wanted to see if there was anything I could do to support him. Plus, I wanted time alone with him to learn more about these conflicts with Edna. Almost everyone had strife in relationships. But mostly they're in private. I brought just my boy along for this trip, giving him some relief from Trixie. Mom should have been able to handle just one dog. I turned off the car and looked at Max. His head lifted, preparing for our visit. A somber expression, knowing this was not playtime.

"Let's get your leash attached and head in."

Max stood obediently and I hooked his collar. I opened my door and he leapt across my lap and out, eager to get going to our destination.

We approached the screen door, the interior door open. I knocked. "Ralph, it's Chloe."

After about two minutes, when I was just about to give up, Ralph appeared at the door. "Sorry, Chloe. I didn't hear you. I was in the bedroom."

"No worries."

Max and I entered, and I gave Ralph a hug while Max hugged my leg. I reached down to pat him and assure him.

Ralph turned and walked down the hallway. "Come on into the kitchen where we can talk."

Max and I followed him on the route that would have taken us to the backyard. It must be excruciating to stay in the home where your loved one passed away.

"Have a seat." Ralph gestured to the dining table, then took the chair at the head of the table.

I took the place to Ralph's left. Max ventured away into the kitchen. He sat as still as a statue with his nose pointed to the countertop.

"Ralph, I'm so sorry for your loss. I'd like to help in any way I can. If you need someone to go through Edna's things at some point, I'm here for you." I peered at Max, who hadn't budged. I guess as long as he wasn't destroying anything, it was OK.

"Thanks, that would be great. There's definitely a lot of paperwork. And a lot of her personal things. I'll let you know when the time is right."

Ralph's shoulders slumped over, and there were bags under his eyes. He must have still been in shock. I think we all were.

"Sorry if I'm nosy." I leaned forward. "Did Edna have any underlying health conditions? Mom suspects her heart may have given out." Max now gave a whimper so light I almost didn't hear it. I ignored the interruption to our conversation.

Ralph shook his head. "No, not really. I just can't figure out how this happened. I really want some answers."

Max now doubled the volume of his whine.

"Ralph, I know the cops will ask this too, if they haven't already. You weren't home when Caroline came over to take her to the Garden Club and found her?"

Another whimper from Max. I glared at him to be quiet.

"No, I was buying parts for the old Studebaker. I wanted to have it running well for the car show coming up in Emerald Hills. I know the person closest to the victim is always a suspect. That hurts even more."

Was there a way to confirm his alibi? Max pierced the air with a yip. With that, I got up to bring him back to the dining room. On the kitchen counter I spied a box of gingersnaps labeled *Caroline's Confections*.

Ralph chuckled when he saw the focus of Max's attention. "Your boy sure does have a sweet tooth."

No doubt about that. Ginger seemed to be his preference. I'd learned after last Christmas that I had to locate my gingerbread men even farther out of reach than I thought. I still remember Max returning to the living room after what I thought was him going to get a drink of water or some kibble. Instead, his breath smelled of gingerbread. I went into the kitchen, and darned if one of the little guys wasn't missing and not a crumb of evidence remained, except his ginger-smelling breath.

"You don't know the half of it."

I looked at my dog. *I don't know, Max.* Why would Ralph have a box of Caroline's gingerbread cookies? Was she over here for some reason? Was there a spark being rekindled? Even before Edna's death? Did Ralph and Edna's fighting cause him to seek comfort from someone else?

I called Max over to sit next to me. Message received.

I shifted in my chair. "I'm sorry if I'm the bearer of news, but I think you should know, there's lots of gossip going around about public disagreements between you and Edna. That's fueling the fire of speculation that maybe you had something to do with her death." I let that big, ugly statement sit right there out in the open. I hoped with my open-ended statements I'd get him to keep talking.

"I know," Ralph said. "I wish we hadn't done it in public, but sometimes my temper gets the best of me. Especially when I learned she'd been taken advantage of. I was trying to protect her, but she was so fiercely independent. And the stubborn woman would never admit when she was wrong."

He was on a roll now. If Max could be patient just a bit longer, he'd be in for a real treat later. I needed to follow this line of questioning through to its conclusion.

"Who took advantage of her?"

Ralph looked out the window, pausing before his answer. It took him so long to start talking again I thought this might be the end of the line.

"It was some supposedly long-lost nephew of hers asking for money. At first, she sent him a one-time, small amount. Then it became ongoing. I thought she was being scammed. I was convinced he was taking advantage of her, and I wanted her to stop sending the money. Her big heart couldn't bear cutting him off, so she kept doing it. Then, one day she told me she discontinued the payments. I never knew why, but I was proud of her for setting boundaries." His hands had migrated to his lap. Out of the corner of my eye I saw them clenching and unclenching. Poor guy, enough grilling for now. Max and I had some work to do to put together the pieces of this puzzle. I felt like I was leaving with more questions than answers.

CHAPTER FOURTEEN

"**M**om, I'm going to be in the back during the meeting, continuing the review of the books."

"OK, Chloe. And keep those unruly dogs under wraps. I don't know why you have to bring them everywhere with us. They don't behave and they smell." Mom headed to the front of the room to sit with her friend Loretta and wait for the Garden Club meeting to start. I was pretty sure the main reason Mom was a member was for the gossip factor. It had become her hobby. Today's meeting agenda was to plan the fundraiser for the year. At the election, Caroline overran everyone into naming a scholarship in Edna's name. A nice idea, but it really should have been voted on. The ladies began to gather in the room and join their cliques. If I closed my eyes, I'd swear I was in a middle school lunchroom.

"Welcome, club members." Caroline sounded very official and quite full of herself. "Please settle in and we'll get started in a minute. I'll gavel the meeting to order when we're ready."

Since I wouldn't be around to see it all, I'd no doubt continue getting play-by-plays from Mom on our calls.

"I've got some pastries from the shop here for everyone," Caroline continued.

Mom and Loretta glanced at each other again. "Do we have to pay for them?" Loretta asked.

"No, silly. The club dues cover the costs," Caroline said. Another glance between Mom and Loretta.

"Don't you think we should vote on where we spend money?" Loretta asked. "I mean, it's nice to have the treats, but we don't have a lot of money to spend. And maybe it could better be used elsewhere." Loretta continued her challenge of Caroline.

"Well, I was just trying to do something nice. Brighten the mood for everyone after the somber meeting we had last time."

Sandy sprang to Caroline's defense. "It's not that much. And Caroline's right. It's nice to have the treats for us."

"Sure. More money in her pocket. But nothing to show for the club," Pearl chimed in.

"This isn't about money, Pearl. I'd think you would know me by now," Caroline said. "I'm going to call the meeting to order and get past this nonsense." She slammed the gavel so hard I thought the head was going to fly off. The sound startled the pups enough for them to jump up to attention, ready for the intruder.

What was behind Caroline's defensiveness? Was she really in as much debt as the rumors indicated? The minutes of the last meeting were read. Caroline's color returned and she beamed at the recap of her victorious election.

Emboldened, she continued. "The main thing for us today is to decide on the fundraising plan. We decided last time some of the money would go to a scholarship in Edna's name toward a student planning to study agriculture."

Silence from the crowd. Everyone seemed worn out from all the pregame activities.

"Who has ideas?" Caroline continued.

"I think we should do the plant sale," Loretta said. "It's always brought in good money in the past. And plants are what the club's all about." Loretta bravely forged ahead.

"Sure." Caroline tapped her chin. "That worked OK. But we need to think bigger. What's going to maximize our revenue? I'm thinking we expand what we're selling to other items." Caroline barreled on.

"Caroline," Loretta said, "we need to stay true to our mission. Agriculture. I say we stick with the plants."

"Stop thinking small. This is about honoring Edna and providing for the kids." Caroline countered.

Nobody bought that line. Something else was going on.

I tried my best to bury my nose in the hotel books. But the tension in the room was palpable. I'd have to return to them later. The meeting continued with volleys back and forth on the fundraising plan until Caroline wore everyone down. Plants plus a lot of other items that had nothing to do with plants. Caroline gaveled the meeting to a close, looking smug with another victory. No doubt they'd make more money with her plan. But it did dilute their purpose.

The ladies milled about in their cliques, whispering.

"You know, I think she just wants more money to funnel into her business." Loretta loaded a handful of gingersnaps into her purse. "I hear it isn't doing well. I mean, charging us for pastries. That's tacky. We paid for these, ladies. Be sure to get your fair share."

The whisper was loud enough for Caroline to hear, and she belted out, "How dare you! My business is doing very well."

Loretta raised her nose in the air. "I doubt it. You used to have full cases of products. Now you're lucky if you have ten percent. And adding all that other crap for sale in your shop. You're obviously in trouble."

I was pretty sure Loretta hit the nail on the head. The place looked rundown, neglected, and more like a swap meet.

"Mom, let's go."

Trixie and Max stood at attention ready to leave. We all wanted out of this mess. It was a no-win situation.

"Just a minute, Chloe. You and the dogs can go. I'll be out soon."

No way she'd miss a minute of the action.

"So what if I added to my store? It's a good business decision," Caroline said.

"Be honest for once, Caroline," Loretta said. "Pretty sure it won't kill you. And we can all see the truth anyway. Who knows? Maybe you offed Edna so you could take her place and use the money from the Garden Club to save your business."

"Yeah, or maybe you thought you could get Ralph back with Edna out of the picture," Pearl added.

That cracked Caroline open. Tears formed and dropped onto her cheek. She slumped. "I had nothing to do with Edna's death. And I resent you implying I did just to save my business."

"Well, it was you that found her. Just sayin'." Loretta was not backing down. I don't know if she believed it. But she was out to hurt.

Caroline advanced to blubbering. Sandy handed her a tissue. "I can't believe you suspect me of something so horrific. Yes, my business is struggling. I admit that. But I would never have harmed Edna. It was probably that stupid dog of hers that made her trip and hit her head." Sandy continued consoling her. As we passed by, I overheard Sandy whisper to Caroline, "No one knows more than I do how hard you work for this club and the sacrifices you've made. The sacrifices we've *both* made so you can win."

"Never mind that, Sandy. You just don't understand."

Sandy looked like the bride left at the altar. Caroline grabbed the remainder of the pastries and stormed out the door. Without a word, we all exited the room, filing out through store. From the corner of my eye, I spotted Caroline returning the unused pastries to the sales display case. How bad was her debt for the business that she had to recycle food?

CHAPTER FIFTEEN

I was not looking forward to today. Edna's memorial service was scheduled for the Shady Acres Cemetery. It was a small, overgrown place in town that would probably have given Edna a fit if she realized she was going to be there. The grass was usually a foot high, unless there was a service planned. Mom and I had a relatively silent morning, unlike most since I'd arrived. I think Edna's death had emphasized her mortality even more, putting it front and center. She was scared and today would stress her out. I prepped for an unusually high amount of snark. We left the pups at home and headed to the service. The silence continued. I pulled into the parking lot at the cemetery next to a few other cars that had arrived.

We left the car and headed toward the service location. Still not a peep from Mom. I'd just leave her to her thoughts for now. I was so pleased that, despite Edna's gruff exterior, someone had taken care to provide her with a beautiful presentation of those garden flowers that she loved. Several chairs had been placed in rows. Mom led us to the front at the left end. Even in her grief, she didn't want to miss a beat of gossip. I hoped even those who weren't the best of friends with Edna would still pay their respects. She was owed that. In continued silence, the remainder of the chairs filled in. About ten minutes after noon, the preacher approached the front of the group and began the service. Mom grabbed my hand and squeezed tight. I returned the gesture. Thankfully, I'd brought a large supply of tissues as Mom's sniffles had already begun. The preacher's words were kind, as they always were when we looked back at someone's life.

Out of the corner of my eye, I spotted motion in the parking lot. A late arrival disturbed the solemn ceremony. I didn't recognize the person. It was a younger man who made his way to the back row of chairs and took a seat on the end. Mom's sniffles flowed a steady stream. Not that I wanted her to suffer, but perhaps this reminder of an imminent death would soften her disposition, even just a little. She leaned over and whispered, "Who is that guy?"

Not wanting to disturb anyone, I turned to her and shrugged. She turned around, got a better look at him, and returned my shrug. Oh, well. Fodder for gossip at another time. I was shocked. Mom knew everyone and everything going on in town but didn't recognize the man. Odd.

The preacher finished up. Mom sniffled a final time and deposited the tissue into her purse. We held hands throughout the entire service. She got up and led me toward the car. "Now I'll never get that ring her father promised me." Even in her grief, she couldn't let it go that Edna kept the ring.

The plan was for all of us to go to Caroline's after the service. I hoped the sting of accusation had lessened since the fundraiser planning meeting. But nothing ever died down in this place. It only amped up. We arrived at the passenger door of my car and Mom let go of my hand.

"Chloe, that guy who was late looked familiar. But I don't know who it is."

I opened the door and Mom got in, then I went around and got in the driver's side.

"Not sure. I don't know many people here anymore."

I started the car and we headed to Caroline's. I just prayed the gathering didn't devolve into a gossip-fest. A girl could hope, couldn't she?

The parking lot looked like the whole town was in attendance for the reception in remembrance of Edna. Caroline's back room would be packed. I squeezed my car into one of the last available spots. I got out and scurried to the passenger side to assist Mom. I warned her not to wear those heels, especially for the graveside service. That's all I needed. For her to end up topsy-turvy in front of all her friends. She insisted the shoes went with the dress and somehow we avoided the incident. She hoisted herself out with a grunt. I stood by in case I needed to catch her. I was relieved our route was a paved path leading to the store. We joined the flow of people funneling into Caroline's. There was a low rumble of under-the-breath conversations going on. I hadn't seen as many people in here since I'd returned to town. The same pitiful, sparse pastry display cried out for attention. Who knew how old those things were? Likely the amount of sugar preserved them for eternity. We all passed through the store into the meeting room. I spotted Buzz and Pearl to the side as we entered and gave a small wave and head nod. People milled about in an uncomfortable presence.

"Mom, I'm going to say hi to Buzz. Do you want to find a seat?"

She selected a table mid-room. A prime location to watch the show. I sat my purse in the chair next to her and wove my way through the bodies to reach Buzz.

"This is quite a turnout, huh?" I said.

"Yeah, it's nice," Buzz said. "Though I'm a bit skeptical that some people are just here for the gossip. Nonetheless, I'm glad to see it. How's your mom doing?"

I looked him in the eye. "Judging by the usual amount of tart to her comments? She's doing OK. I think it reminds her, and all of us, of our own mortality. And that's sobering."

"You got that right. Hey, we really need to get that golf game in. I don't care if you're rusty. It'll be fun."

I chuckled. "Rusty? That would be an improvement. Get ready for a triple-digit score."

He quietly snickered. "You know, even the guys I play with regularly have that issue. So you'll fit right in."

"OK everyone." Oddly, Caroline had a pretty huge grin on her face. "We're about to get started. If you'd like something to eat, you need to come into the store to buy that." I could see dollar signs in her eyes as she scanned the crowd, calculating probably the biggest boost to her business in a while. Not that she should provide the food free of charge. But I'd bet she offered her place so she'd get the business. I'd help her out. And the pastries, at least when fresh, were pretty good. I navigated back to the table with Mom to see that Brittany had joined her.

"Hi, Aunt Chloe."

"Hi, Britt. I'm going to get something to eat. Would either of you like something?"

"I'm not giving that woman a dime of my hard-earned money." I'd expect nothing less of a response from Mom.

"Yes, please," Brittany said. "And, Aunt Chloe. Do you know that guy who came late to the service? I didn't recognize him."

"Not sure, exactly. But I think it was the same guy who checked into the hotel yesterday. I mean, he looks a lot different. But I can't shake the feeling that there's something familiar about him."

"The person at the hotel had long hair, sloppy clothes. It wasn't him," Mom confidently said.

She would probably know. She had a keen eye for details if it had anything to do with the theater that was this town.

Loretta, overhearing our conversation, chimed in, "I saw him at the bank too." Seriously, there was no way you'd ever get away with anything in this town. They didn't need to find the budget for the town cop. They could just crowdsource the investigation and save a lot of money. "Maybe he's a lawyer. He's all fancy in that suit."

There was a familiarity about him. But probably our stressed brains playing tricks. Without knowing the real reason for Edna's death, speculation continued to abound. We needed answers, and fast. If much more time passed without clarity, we'd probably have a full-blown riot on our hands.

CHAPTER SIXTEEN

This was not going to be easy. Edna and Ralph's house looked like an antique store had exploded. Don't get me wrong, there were many beautiful pieces displayed in every room, on every surface. I partially reconsidered my volunteering to help Ralph sort through Edna's things. This would be tedious. But maybe I'd get some more answers to the outstanding questions around Edna's death. We'd need a strategy to get through this in a timely manner. The only possible family of Edna's that I knew of was the nephew mentioned by Ralph. First thing was we'd organize and inventory Edna's things. We decided we'd each take a room and tackle it, but we might need reinforcements. Ralph hauled in stacks of varying sized boxes and supplies to start packing.

I returned to the living room and planned to go through the paperwork on Edna's desk. Before I settled in, I let the pups outside to expend energy. I needed them calm while we went through Edna's things. I strolled around the beautiful garden while the dogs explored. They raced back and forth at top speed. We'd worked our way to the opposite end of the yard and were making the return trip. Passing by Edna's gnomes from the opposite angle as I had the other day, I noticed the missing gnome, *Speak No Evil*, had fallen under a bush. I grabbed it and returned it to its place next to *See No Evil, Hear No Evil*. I was ashamed that I'd even considered that Mom had stolen the gnome from Edna to complete her own collection. Even with all of her warts, she wasn't a thief.

I had to corral the dogs before there was any more damage. They panted with tongues out to the sides of their mouths. I found a couple of bowls in the kitchen and filled them with water. The slurping continued on for at least five minutes. Now I could focus on my task at hand. I grabbed a stack of papers from Edna's desk and sat on the couch. I began to separate them into piles. Bills to pay. Junk mail. Miscellaneous. I quickly completed that task and returned to her desk for round two. Max joined me in his normal puzzle-solving position, ready to dig in. Before we could access Edna's account to pay the bills, we'd have to speak with an attorney for guidance. At least I'd be prepared for that meeting with what we needed. I cracked open the book to see what I was dealing with. Nothing could be as messed up as the hotel books. I perused the entries until I got to those indicating she'd sent money to her supposed nephew, as Ralph had shared. It had been almost four months since she'd done that and every month prior there was a pretty significant amount. Her payments to the alleged nephew had continued to increase over time. Max placed his paw on the book, looked at me and raised an eyebrow. I needed another set of eyes on this to validate what I was seeing.

I traipsed down the hall to the bedroom, where Ralph was putting Edna's things into a box. "Ralph, question for you. I know you said Edna had been paying this guy who said he was her nephew."

"Yep. She finally cut him off a few months ago. That went on for too long, in my opinion. But it was her money."

"It looks from the entries over the last year or so that she'd increased the amount she was giving him."

"He kept giving her bigger sob stories. And she bought it."

"Why did she stop paying him?"

"You know, I'm not exactly sure. Maybe all of my badgering finally sunk in. When I first learned of it, she was extremely defensive and basically told me to butt out. It was none of my business. That was true."

I fanned myself with the bills. "Do you think she finally saw the light?"

"Yeah, she was stubborn." Ralph stuffed some shoes into the box. "It finally got to be her idea to cut him off. She told me after one of the final calls with him that she'd had it. He couldn't explain what he'd done with the money. It was always some BS story or another. I think it really hurt her that she'd been taken advantage of."

"Well, I'm glad she finally got to that point with him. You can't help someone who won't help themselves. No matter how heartbreaking their situation is." The bedroom was filled to the gills as the rest of the house, the dresser covered with every kind of jewelry. "Edna has some really beautiful pieces here."

"She sure does. I think most of it's costume jewelry and a couple of fine pieces."

The ring with the giant ruby looked suspiciously like the same one Mom claimed Edna's father had promised to her. I closed the book and returned to my tasks in the living room.

Trixie had assumed the dead bug position, her little snout snoring like a chain saw. Max preoccupied himself chewing on a piece of paper. That little rascal. I learned early on I had a canine paper shredder on my hands and took precautions to keep everything out of his reach. I went over retrieved the soggy paper. He clenched harder. "Max," I said softly. His eyebrows raised, still not releasing his prize. He shook his head *no*. "Max," I repeated. He slowly unclamped his jaw. I held the paper at the very edge, seeing that it was a receipt from the Emerald Hills Extended Stay Motel.

Where in the world did he discover this? It could only belong to Edna or Ralph. Did this confirm Ralph and Caroline were indeed having a tryst? I didn't want to believe it, but there was the evidence, right before my eyes. Poor Edna. I tucked the moist piece of paper into the books. I'd have to deal with that later. Again, more questions than answers. Was that nephew the real deal? On one hand I'd hate for that to be true and him to be the only living relative of Edna's who inherited her things. Especially after taking advantage of her. On the other hand, if she had no other family, I really wanted to make sure her things went to good homes. We'd have to see what the attorney said.

I found a blank notebook and began making a task list. *Another note to self: Be more organized with my stuff and directions for when I pass.* Being a widow with no kids, I didn't want any questions or extra stress about what my family was to do with my things. Especially my little buddy, Max. But we'd just have to hope my death wasn't soon enough where Max got left behind. And, for now, Trixie. Could I keep her too? Temporary custody was tolerable, but a permanent companion? I'd have to think long and hard about doing that to Max.

"Ralph," I hollered down the hallway.

He emerged from the bedroom.

"Yeah, Chloe? What is it?"

"I just got a call from Mom. I have to head back to the hotel. I'll check in with you later on next steps." He looked spent. I empathized deeply with him going through a loved one's things after they passed. When I had to do that with Frank's belongings, it was unbearable. Thankfully I had several friends who shared the burden. I was still pretty peeved at Ralph for his tryst with Caroline, though. I just hoped if they were going to advance their relationship, they'd wait an appropriate amount of time. I signaled the pups it was time to go. They jumped up and the race for the front seat was on. I was pretty sure if Trixie could talk I'd have heard her call shotgun. Max waited for the door to open, knowing he'd have no chance at the front seat.

I hated to lie to Ralph, but until I knew for sure I couldn't accuse anyone and destroy reputations. You never lived those down in this town.

CHAPTER SEVENTEEN

I picked up a bite to eat at the cute little drive-up burger joint, then arrived at the hotel only to find Brittany's car in the parking lot. I always hoped every time I drove up that there'd be more cars there of people who wanted to stay. The three of us piled out of the car and headed inside. I'd brought extra supplies for the pups to keep at the office since we were spending so much time there. They were treated as if they were the royal guests themselves.

I walked into the office. "Hi Britt. Hi Mom. We're back."

"How was it?" Mom asked. "Did you find out anything new? How is Ralph doing? I still don't trust him." She gave me the third degree as if I were a suspect.

"Whoa, Mom. Ralph is still pretty shaken, of course." I couldn't share any of Edna's business with her. No way I'd fuel the fire of gossip.

"Well, Buzz better call pretty quickly with an update. He promised I'd be the first to know." Mom demanded her due. Mabel was nothing if not always in the know.

"I'm sure he will." Little did she know, she might have a front row seat to more than she bargained for. I sat down to eat my lunch before all hell broke loose.

My phone started to vibrate and I saw Buzz's name on the caller ID. I'd called him after leaving Ralph's with my theory about Edna. He was pretty skeptical but said he'd check it out. There was really no other explanation for all of the clues I'd put together. I secretly think he was a bit embarrassed I got to that point before he did. Since his retirement, he'd lost a step.

"Who was that, Chloe?" Mom asked. Yep, right on cue.

"It was a friend from back home. I guess there was a storm last night and when she went to check on my house, a part of the fence was down."

She nodded, buying my lie.

Buzz warned me that we might be in the eye of the storm any minute. The call from my friend Cindy at the bank tipped me off that Arthur was trying to get into Edna's accounts.

Truth be told, I was pretty nervous after Buzz's call. I mean, could the nephew be dangerous? We didn't have anything to protect ourselves here. Although, setting Mom up with a gun had all kinds of disaster written all over it. Maybe a security system would better suit us. I attempted normalcy while continuing my lunch meal.

The door squeaked open. I jumped about a foot and almost choked on my burger. The clean-cut guy from the memorial service entered. He had all of his bags in hand. Brittany eyed me. *See, it was him!* Up close, I could definitely see it too.

I gave a small nod. I needed to act as normal as I could. "Can I help you?"

"Yes, I'm checking out." He placed his key on the desk.

"Thank you so much for staying. Will you be returning anytime soon? We have a discount for your second visit." I totally just made that up on the spot. I heard the faint sound of gravel crunching. Oh, please be Buzz. And please be someone with a gun in case this guy goes bonkers.

"No thanks. I won't be back."

There was nothing more I could do to delay. He turned and sped to the door like his hair was on fire. He opened it to greet Detective Jansen on the other side. I heard a squeal and a clap. I turned and gave Mom a look. This was serious. She continued to applaud like she was at a live show. Oh well. I'd let her have this. Better than a phone call from Buzz, it was a front row seat to the arrest. This would be gossip fodder for quite a while.

Detective Jansen stepped inside and grabbed Arthur's arm, turning it behind him to be cuffed. He dropped his bag from his other hand and the detective placed it in the second cuff.

"You're under arrest for the murder of Edna Gregory." Detective Jansen continued mirandizing him.

He led him out to his car and Buzz followed with the travel bag. The three of us went to the door to watch. The detective tucked the nephew's head and guided him into the back of his car. Already in the backseat of the detective's car was a man old enough to be Arthur's father.

"Why are there two of them?" Mom demanded. "What's going on? That's Walter!"

"Would you like to do the honors, Chloe?" Buzz asked.

Mom looked at me. "Chloe, what do you know about this? You mean you lied to me? And why is Walter being arrested? I mean, he was a terrible accountant. But, I didn't think it was anything illegal." She continued staring at me and waited for my answer.

"Mom, I didn't want to accuse someone if it wasn't factual. And in the end, you had a front row seat."

Appeased, she took a seat.

I could see the wheels turning in her head about how she was going to regale the Garden Club with the story. "When I was helping Ralph go through Edna's things I learned how Walter was blackmailing Edna. I could tell from her records that she'd borrowed some money from the Garden Club one time but paid it back. She even pawned that ring you said Lloyd promised to you. Eventually, she must have turned things around financially because I saw the ring had returned to her bedroom dresser. Walter must have discovered she took the Garden Club money and was blackmailing her after she fired him. The embarrassment would have been horrific for her reputation. She cut him off and he must have been trying to get her to keep paying. He couldn't come to town because everyone knows him. So he sends his nephew, Arthur, to spy for him and figure out how to get into Edna's accounts."

"Chloe, I knew that hippie was bad business. Didn't I tell you that? And that horrible man, Walter. I'm pretty sure the only reason Sandy recommended him was because he's her cousin."

"Yes, you did Mom, but for a different reason. Anyway, I found a receipt at Edna's that was for the same place Arthur had been staying in Emerald Hills. Or, more accurately, Max found it. Arthur must have dropped it when he went over there. With Ralph having an alibi for that time, I knew he couldn't have killed Edna. Arthur may have just been planning to intimidate her but ending up hitting her with the gazing globe. Buzz told me they found a piece of it in her skull."

"I have to get on the phone to the Garden Club." Mom ran toward the phone. "They won't believe this. We might just have to have a special meeting so I can tell everyone what happened." Mom would ride this high for quite a while. She was already on the phone to Caroline. I hadn't seen her this pepped up in a while.

CHAPTER EIGHTEEN

Somehow, Mom had convinced Caroline to hold a special meeting of the Garden Club. It probably didn't take much persuasion. Everyone wanted to hear the details of the arrest. I suspected there might be some embellishments to the story, but this was Mom's moment. One of those times she loved being the center of attention. I was happy for her. If she enjoyed this, who was I to poop all over it? I'd vowed never to join a meeting again, but seeing Mom's performance was worth breaking my promise. The pups and I took our usual spot in the back of Caroline's meeting room. I wanted nothing to do with the spotlight. Caroline had even donated treats for the occasion. From generosity or an improved business plan? I wasn't sure. But she'd created a beautiful cupcake with a peony design on top. It looked as lovely as one of Edna's prize-winning flowers. For what seemed like hours, Mom regaled the crowd with the play-by-play of the takedown of Walter and his nephew, Arthur. She was quite the storyteller. How much more exciting and dire would it become with each telling? There wasn't much garden business going on, so Caroline gaveled the special meeting to a close.

Mom came to sit at my table. "Wow. My heart is still racing from the excitement of yesterday. A real-life criminal in our little town."

"Yeah. That was something all right. I'm so glad they got him. But why do people have to do that to others?" Having heard stories from Frank for decades as a police officer, I knew there was evil in the world. I'd never understand how you could hurt someone that way. "Buzz just called. He let me know that Ralph found a will in Edna's paperwork. Her things will be sold and a permanent scholarship set up for the agriculture students. Those blackmailing scum balls won't get a dime. Mom, we should probably get home to finish up getting everything ready for tonight."

Our family dinner had taken a far back seat to the murder. Mom wanted to return to the times in the past when all of her kids were together. Without Harrison, it wouldn't be the same. No chance he'd come for a visit while I was here. It might just have to be another time.

"Why are you worrying so much, Chloe? It'll all come together just fine. I mean, it has before. This will be no different."

"OK, Mom." We all got up and headed out to the car. I was still exhausted from the events of yesterday.

We settled into our seats for the ride home. "Chloe, I'm hoping Harrison can come for a visit soon. With you back in town I just need him for my family to be complete again."

Max gave me a knowing look. He really did sense all of my moods. I smiled warmly at my boy. His companionship meant the world to me. No expectations. Well, maybe some that had to do with ginger cookies. But he gave so much more than he took. If only I could do the same. I'd work on that. He was even generous in tolerating Trixie. No small feat.

"Maybe we'll try to arrange for another time." I hoped to appease her.

"Chloe, this is your home. And with Frank gone, you have nothing left there anymore. You need to come back. It would be so great if we could run the hotel together."

Maybe I will, Mom. Maybe I will.

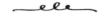

VIOLETS AND VENGEANCE

A TREEHOUSE HOTEL COZY MYSTERY
(BOOK 2)

SUE HOLLOWELL

CHAPTER ONE

B uttercup Bungalow began to look like my vision of what the Cedarbrook Treehouse Hotel could be. Guests should expect staying in a treehouse would be an adventure with fun and whimsy sprinkled in. When I arrived to help Mom untangle the books so we could list the hotel for sale, I never expected to stay this long. My dutiful companion Max and I originally stayed at Mom's when I returned to town. But I needed my space. And staying in a room at the hotel would give me a better chance to renovate it the way it deserved.

The hotel in its prime was a destination for many. Rooms were booked a year in advance. The place was a hub for many functions in this small town. If only I could get it even partially returned to that glory, I'd consider myself successful. I was handy with a toolbelt and not afraid to get my hands dirty. Plus, fixing up the rooms was kind of like solving a puzzle—replacing what's missing, fixing problems—and I'd always been good at puzzles.

Today, I was decorating the interior of this place. I'd gone to the stores in Emerald Hills to find yellow-themed items to go along with buttercups. I purchased material with yellow flowers to hang up as curtains and some paint to cover the nightstand in a matching golden hue. The place had already brightened with those two changes. The wooden walls of the treehouses darkened the interior and required creativity to style and lighten it up. I wanted the feel of happiness, joy, and relaxation for all of the units. Spending time with Mom while fixing the place up had become enjoyable. The times we worked together, I appreciated her sense of whimsy. Although she insisted we display some of those garden gnomes she collected. I just couldn't go there.

My phone chimed and I saw Pearl's Pooch Pampering on the caller ID. I'd taken Max and Trixie to get groomed earlier this morning, and it looked like they were calling to let me know they were ready to be picked up. My sister, Joey, one of us triplets, was a part-time cashier there when she wasn't waitressing at Smokehouse Restaurant. She had several family members living with her, so she held down multiple jobs to try and make ends meet.

"Hi, Joey. Are the pooches ready to be picked up?"

Silence on the other end. I thought maybe the connection was bad. Out here at the hotel, sometimes reception was spotty, at best.

"Joey? Can you hear me?" I heard sniffles. "Joey, is that you?"

"Chloe, you won't believe it," she said and sniffled.

At least we had a connection now. And yes, I probably would believe it. My time in Cedarbrook had been more than eventful. Edna's murder had thrown this place into a tizzy. And with that resolved, the excitement began to disappear. Plus, out of all my siblings, Joey had the most drama. She had quite a few kids and grandkids, and someone or another was always in trouble. Bless her heart, though, she always retained a positive outlook, no matter how many times she had to bail someone out of jail.

"What's going on? Are the pups ready to be picked up?" My faithful companion, Max, had fur that went on for days. His buff-colored cocker spaniel coat needed constant care or we'd be in for a rat's nest like no other. Sticks and leaves adhered to him like Velcro. Sometimes when I peeled them off I had a pile of debris the size of a small shrub. Trixie was new to our family. When Mom's friend Edna died, her boyfriend didn't want to keep the little dog. She was a bit of a handful, but her companionship was unparalleled. I'd taken her for a bit while we sorted things out with Edna, and by the end of that time, Trixie and Mom had become fast friends. To say I was shocked was an understatement. That Trixie could soften Mom's demeanor was truly amazing. Now Mom rarely went anywhere without her.

"No," Joey said. This was like pulling teeth.

"Is it Mom?" I asked. Mom was in her eighties. She retained great health for that age, just had the usual aches and pains of an older body.

"No. It's Violet," she said. Violet and Joey had no love lost between them. But really, anyone in town could say that about themselves and Violet.

"Did you guys get into it again?" I asked. Silence. I was sure I'd lost the connection now. I looked at my phone and saw surprisingly we were still getting a pretty strong signal. It was about time to head to Pearl's anyway to get the dogs. It was a good time for a break from all of the buttercup yellow, as cheery as that was. "Joey, I'll be there soon." I listened for a few seconds and didn't hear a disconnect.

"Chloe." Joey started crying even more. "I don't know what happened."

I beelined out the door to my car. Pearl was owner of the dog spa and had a pretty level head. "Is Pearl there?"

"I don't know where she is. She went on an errand but wouldn't say what it was."

Clearly I wasn't going to get any more information from Joey on the call. I threw my purse onto the passenger seat and started the car. "I'm on my way."

Pearl's Pooch Pampering was located on the main street of this small town. Rows of quaint little shops lined both sides of the road. Pearl's was pretty much smack dab in the center. Most stores didn't have lots of parking, but you didn't need much in a town with a population of two thousand. Pearl's was no exception. With the amount of business she did, she had tried to expand, but it infringed on the neighboring businesses and was a no-go. Her shop was packed every day. Pet pampering must be a billion-dollar industry, based on how well Pearl did. I found a spot a few blocks away and speed-walked to Pearl's, preparing myself for the unexpected. I heard raised voices before I even got to the front door. The scene through the glass door did not look right. I slowly opened the door. Joey sat in a chair along the wall in the waiting room, her head down, sobbing into a handful of tissues. On the opposite side of the room, Judy, Violet's sister-in-law, was on the phone. She posed business-like in her standard matching pantsuit. We made eye contact and she told the person on the other end of the line she had to go. I wondered what business Judy had here. She was proudly a cat person and let everyone know it. Mom had said the last time her friend Caroline was at Judy's for dinner, her felines even sat at the table and ate off of plates.

"Chloe, Violet's dead," Judy proclaimed. She gestured to the other side of the large display of pet supplies.

My hand flew to my mouth. "Oh my God! What happened?" I asked the room. I'd take an explanation from anyone right now. Violet's body was situated on her left side, facing the wall, her head covered by stuffed plushy dog toys.

"Were you calling an ambulance?" I asked Judy, and navigated to the chair next to Joey.

"What good would that do?" Judy replied as she paced. Judy glanced at Joey, paused, then said, "I found her like that when I came in."

Joey looked up, obviously distraught. "I heard the bell ring and thought it was Violet coming to get Sasha. You know she griped every time about how we trimmed her poodle. And she thought the prices were outrageous for what she was getting. I just couldn't take it anymore." Joey dipped her head again. She extended her left arm toward Violet. "I came into the room and found Judy standing over Violet."

My heart sank. I'd never known Joey to be violent. But I guess we never truly knew what people could do under pressure.

I sat next to Joey and grabbed her hand. "Joey," I said, locking into her gaze. My shoulders slumped.

She shook her head no. I would have to take her word for it until I knew the truth. "Where's Sasha now?"

She pointed to the back through a swinging door.

"Judy, would you call Buzz and let him know what happened? He'll want to know someone died in his wife's place of business," I said, taking charge of the mayhem. Buzz was our retired town cop. He would get the investigative ball rolling.

Without a word, she pulled her phone out and dialed.

I headed to the back room to locate Sasha, Trixie, and Max, and make sure the place was still standing. They were all chillin' post-grooming from a day at the spa. Max and Trixie sprinted toward me and Sasha continued to lounge. That was good. We'd have to figure out a home for her now. I grabbed the leashes and led my two dogs back to the lobby, skirting the crime scene.

Judy remained on the phone, but it didn't sound like a call to Buzz. She was a busy person, given her position on the town council.

Max sat and refused to budge. "Max, let's go." His soulful brown eyes looked at me with empathy. "I know, boy. We have quite the puzzle on our hands again." Following Max's lead, Trixie lined up right next to him and plopped down.

CHAPTER TWO

The bell on the front door jingled, startling all of us out of our skin. I turned my attention away from Violet to see who joined the fray.

"What's going on?" Pearl had returned from her errand to find the lobby of the dog spa in disarray and a dead body front and center. She stopped just inside the door, looked at me, then looked down at Violet. Her puppy paw earrings swung from side to side.

I tightened my rein on Max's and Trixie's leashes. "I don't exactly know. Judy called Buzz so he can let the police know she arrived in the lobby and found Violet like she is now." It looked like she took a nosedive into the display of dog toys.

Pearl crossed over to Violet and bent down to get a better view. She looked at me again, as if I magically had the answers to the obvious questions. "Where's Sasha?" she said, looking around.

"She's in the back," I said. "I'll wait here until Buzz arrives."

"Whew." Pearl swiped her forehead. "I'm glad she's OK. From day one when Violet bought that poodle, I've been concerned about her welfare. I'd never forgive myself if something happened to that dog on Violet's watch," Pearl said. "She never treated her like the royal pedigree she is."

Judy crossed the room and stood over Violet. "Pearl, we need to talk about the pet parade. Now that I see Violet's out of the way, I think you should take over as the organizer."

Pearl took a seat next to Joey and grabbed her hand. She looked up and frowned. Not a word. The nerve of Judy to carry on in the midst of this tragedy.

"Judy, seriously," I said. "There's just been a death in Pearl's place of business. Can't we postpone this until another time? Obviously, we have more pressing issues to take care of."

Judy moved to the lobby seats. "No, it can't wait," she snapped. "It's one of the biggest events in this town. And we can't postpone talking about it."

Max sidled up to me and sat on my foot. He began furiously scratching his left side. I reached down and placed my hand on him to stop. His heart raced at the same speed as mine. Trixie nonchalantly selected dog toys that surrounded the body one by one and placed them in a pile by the door. That little girl behaved as if she was entitled to everything.

Pearl stood. "I agree with Chloe. I can't think of anything else right now." She groaned and lifted both hands to cover her face. "Having a dead body in my lobby is going to be horrible for business. I never liked Violet, but I wouldn't wish her dead."

Judy looked at her watch and tapped it. "I have to go. Council business calls. I agree that it's horrible that Violet's dead. But the timing couldn't be better." She sighed, like she was ready to be done with the whole thing. "I mean with you in charge, it will bring so much more dignity to our annual pet parade. Violet always had those hairbrained ideas that made Cedarbrook a laughingstock of the county. People would come to the parade just to see how outrageous it became each year. Kids and their animals dressed up each year and wound their way through town. How dignified could it get?"

Joey stood, having gained some composure, and re-entered the conversation. "Where were you when I needed you? You know that every time Violet comes in she wants to argue with me. When you're here, at least you can handle it. I don't get paid enough to take her crap."

Pearl took three steps back, her hands raised in defense. "I had an important errand to run. And it's none of your business. I pay you plenty to be the cashier. I'd think you would be grateful for the job, with your family and all."

Wow, Pearl took direct aim. Joey's chin trembled, and her head bowed. The tension escalated. Now, they both started crying. Pearl went to Joey and enveloped her in a hug. "I'm sorry. I'm just so stressed over this. It might be the end of my business, just like Violet wanted."

Judy was in her own world. "And for some odd reason, Violet would never allow cats in the parade, only those rambunctious dogs. Cats are so much better behaved. Now I'll be able to show off my Fifi and the others for all the world to see." Judy strutted around the lobby, full of herself now that things were finally going her way.

The bell jingled again, launching us all into the atmosphere. Trixie continued piling up her treasures and had bumped into the door. Oblivious to anything other than her mission, she gripped a little kangaroo in her mouth.

"I should probably get these two out of here," I said. I grabbed their leashes and headed for the exit. "Buzz should be here soon." Trixie refused to leave her pile of treasures. I gave another tug to encourage her departure.

"Chloe, wait." Pearl stretched her arms out to plead for my assistance. "You can't leave me here. You have to help figure out who did this or I'll be ruined. Even dead, Violet's going to take me down."

I didn't have time to help Pearl. Taking care of renovating the treehouses with Mom had become my full-time job.

"Please, Chloe, I'm begging you." Pearl literally clasped her hands in prayer and shook them at me. "You know how hard I've worked to build this business."

Max stood, turned, and looked at me. My little buddy aligned with Pearl in her plea. He smiled that wide grin, confirming we were on the case together. Max looked out for his newfound canine pal Sasha, wanting to help find her mom's killer.

"All right, then," Judy practically yelled. She tucked her phone in her purse and tiptoed passed Trixie to avoid any touching of a dog. "We're all set. Pearl takes over the pet parade. I better go let Otis know what's happened. Even though Violet was his sister, that husband of mine couldn't stand the way she drove that pet parade downhill. Now in his position as grand marshal, he can sit tall and proud, knowing we're representing the county well. Ta, ta, all." Judy skirted out the door and left us all stunned. Judy and Otis were nothing alike. I was surprised they were still together. Otis, our town veterinarian, was a mild-mannered, caring individual with no more aspirations than to care for animals.

"Pearl, I'll wait until Buzz gets here to take over." I looked her in the eye. "Don't worry. We'll get to the bottom of this mystery. It'll be OK," I said with much more conviction than I felt. *Max, we've got to launch our puzzle-solving selves into high gear.*

CHAPTER THREE

I was grateful for the distraction of the morning with some new projects around the hotel. Mom and I were working on renovating Cherry Cottage. This particular unit was a two-story with a loft for additional sleeping, and an expansive wrap-around deck on the main level. I found myself enjoying this time with my mom. We were finding new paths in our relationship, developing a real partnership in running the hotel. After the events of the morning at Pearl's, the pups and I picked Mom up at her house and headed to the treehouses. Since I'd moved from Mom's to the Buttercup Bungalow, my attitude about being in Cedarbrook had significantly improved. It didn't hurt that I was secluded in nature and enjoying puzzle time alone with Max, enjoying my classic huckleberry vodka cocktail and a gorgeous sunset. We screamed through those sudoku challenges like they were nothing.

"Mom, let's work on the outside today. I bought some things at the garden store to get us started." We sat in the two Adirondack chairs in front of the treehouse, finishing lunch I'd picked up at Caroline's.

"Great. I have so many ideas for this one." Max rose from his slumber, stood, and stared at me without blinking. His stubby tail didn't move an inch. *I know, boy. I'm not sure what to expect either*. Mom was a member of the garden club. Her yard was presentable and, dare I say, eclectic. She insisted on collecting garden gnomes galore, and they inhabited most every inch of that space. I hoped one day they'd grow on me, but so far no such luck.

We finished our meals, and I headed to the car to retrieve our supplies. "Why don't we start by potting these flowers and placing them next to the base of the tree?" I lugged flower seedlings, potting soil, and pots to our work area next to the chairs.

Mom returned to my car and rummaged around in the supplies. "What else do you have here?" She took out three garden stakes and held them up and examined them. They were each a little old lady bending over and all you could see were her bloomers showing a pattern of cherries. "I'm not seeing anything interesting. You need to be more creative with the designs if we want people to like them." She reached into the middle row of seats, retrieved a large bag, and returned to our work area.

I started by gloving up and locating the three planters equally spaced on the side of the steps that faced the treehouse. I'd have to get some pictures of the finished project and put them on the website to upgrade the looks of the hotel. We were slowly gaining a few more guests at a time, in no small part due to the upgrades we made.

"Mom, if you want, you can place those garden stakes on the other side of the steps. I think there's three or four of them." Max sauntered over to sniff my work. He looked at Mom, tilted his head to the side where his long ears swung, and straightened his tail. I looked around at Mom as she carried the stakes to their new home. "It's OK, boy. You've had an exciting morning. You deserve some relaxation."

"So tell me again what happened at Pearl's?" Mom was an expert at gossip. When it came time for the garden club meeting, she didn't want to miss a detail in regaling her friends.

I poured soil into the second pot. "All that I know right now is that Violet's dead. Judy said she found her that way. Joey said she found Judy over the body. Pearl wasn't there. Frankly, I don't know what to think at this point."

Mom placed one of the garden stakes and started pounding it with a trowel. Max jolted with the noise and barked. *We're all a bit on edge, boy. It's OK.* I stopped what I was doing and crouched next to him. I grabbed an ear in each hand and gave a massaging knead. He relaxed and sat. Mom continued pounding until the stake was firmly in the ground. I rounded the steps to get a better look.

"That looks great. This is going to really look nice, even with just a few touches here."

Mom stood back to admire her handiwork. "It does look good."

Max approached the stake and gave the old lady's bottom an approving sniff.

"I wish Joey didn't have to work so many jobs. She told me about this guy, Wyatt, who does those housing developments. She said he comes into the restaurant a lot and he's really nice." Mom took a seat in one of the chairs.

I kept filling pots with the soil. "Really? That's nice."

"It would be so great if she married him. He could be the one for her. Of course, this thing with Violet won't help her dating prospects at all." Joey had a few "this is the one" moments already in her life. A bit like Mom. I didn't know Wyatt but was hopeful he could be someone good for Joey. She deserved it. I got my trowel and dug a small hole in the center of the soil of the first pot and placed a small, light pink flower inside.

"We'll get this worked out," I said. I filled the second and third pots with flowers. I stood back and admired our work. "This looks better with every addition. I'm going to fill the watering can." I headed up to the office where there was the only outside faucet. Renovating one treehouse at a time was going really well. I returned to our work area to find Mom putting her big bag back into the car. I sprinkled water on each of the three plants. Seeing the beauty really did pick up my spirits. Soon enough I'd have to get going to figure out what happened to Violet. Judy was right. That was going to throw a big wrench into the pet parade.

"Get away from there," Mom said to Max. He had sneaked around the side of the steps to the garden stakes and had lifted his leg. I went over to see what Mom was concerned about. And right in the middle of the cute garden stakes was one of her garden gnomes. A little guy with a green hat, cherries on his head and holding a welcome sigh. Max was peeing all over it. "Chloe, look what he's doing. Can you keep him in check? He always seems to be bothering my gnomes. I don't know what's gotten into him."

I was doing everything I could not to bust a gut laughing. "We didn't agree to re-home your gnomes here." I used my watering can and gave it a shower to clean it off. Max looked at me, head down, eyes up, as if he was being scolded. I reached down to pet him.

"I know. But look how cute they are. They really jazz the place up. And he does fit right in with the cherry theme."

They do something, not sure jazzy is it.

"I can't wait to work on the other places. Making them look better will be really good for business. I should have done this long ago," Mom said.

I concurred. Having projects to spend my time on while I was in town really did give me some purpose.

CHAPTER FOUR

Max and I returned to the scene of the crime. If we didn't have answers soon, Pearl would be right. People in this town would ignite a firestorm of rumors and it would be all over for her business. Max trotted through the doorway as if there hadn't been a recent tragedy here. *Maybe he's remembering all of the good times he and Trixie had.* Pampering with Huckleberry scrubs. Manicures, massages. The works. I would prance too if I had received those treatments.

"Hi Buzz," I said. In high school Buzz and I dated for a while. We had become quite good friends after that. Max walked over and sniffed the spot where Violet had been. He looked up at me, curiosity in his eyes. I went over to Pearl and gave her a hug.

"Hey, there. And how are you doing, boy?" Buzz leaned over and gave Max a good scratching behind his ears. The entire back half of Max's body wiggled and he gave that big, goofy Muppet grin. "You come to check on Pearl?"

I went to the display case and retrieved two bottles of the huckleberry shampoo. "Yeah, plus I needed some supplies. This stuff smells amazing. I'm tempted to use it on myself."

"Right? I'm grateful that people spend more on their dogs than themselves. Keeps Pearl in business," Buzz said.

"But for how long?" Pearl chimed in. She went behind the checkout counter and got a bag for my purchase. "If Violet's badmouthing my place wasn't enough, as a final straw, she had to go and die right in my lobby." Pearl's eyes watered, and she choked out those last few words. She rang up my purchases and loaded them into the bag.

"Any word from Emerald Hills Police Department on the cause of death?" I asked Buzz.

He glanced at Pearl, not wanting to further upset her. He came closer to me and said in a whisper, "It looks like strangulation."

My hand went up to my throat. He shook his head yes. I looked over at Pearl and she busied herself arranging the products on the shelves. I went behind the counter and grasped Pearl's hand.

"We'll get to the bottom of this," I said. She looked up at me, tears overflowing her eyes.

"I didn't hate her and I'd never wish her dead," she blubbered.

I took her in my arms. "I know," I said and patted her back.

The bell on the door jingled and we all jumped. Max yipped. The tension was so thick we could cut it with a knife. Yes, we needed answers, and fast, so we could return to normal small-town life.

Everett Landon bustled through the door with a spring in his step. I looked at Buzz, who had a perplexed look on his face. Certainly Everett was aware that Violet had recently died in this lobby. "Hello, Pearl. What a great day!" Everett almost yelled. "I'm so excited to share some of my new products with you today." He lugged his large supply cases up to the counter.

"Everett, it's not a good day," Pearl mumbled.

He ignored her and began to unpack several bottles and line them up on the counter.

"Everett," Buzz said.

Everett stopped what he was doing and looked at Buzz, then Pearl. "What? Life goes on. You know Violet wasn't a favorite of mine. And I can't say I'm sorry to see her go. But nothing I can do about that now."

He picked up where he left off and emptied his bag onto the counter. A couple of the bottles rolled onto the floor. Max sniffed Everett's hand as he reached for the wayward shampoo bottle.

"Whose dog is this? Can you get him away from me?" Everett asked.

Max growled. Always the most accurate judge of character. Everett's crass attitude toward Violet and Max was not winning him any new business. Max got closer to Everett and his left rear leg began to raise.

"Max." I patted my thigh to call him over. Not that I wouldn't approve of him peeing on Everett, who deserved it. But probably not a good habit to condone. He tipped his head down and stopped mid-leg raise. "Max." He dropped his leg and came to stand right by me. He gave a low growl. *I agree, Max. A pet product supply salesman should totally be more of a dog person.*

"I'm sorry, Pearl," Everett conceded. "It must be hard for you that it happened here. But you have to admit, it's better for both of our businesses that Violet's gone. She'd been complaining for years how the huckleberry products tinted Sasha's coat purple. They do no such thing. I'm sure her negative reviews have cost me a lot of business, and you as well." Everett retrieved the bottles from the floor and arranged everything on the counter in preparation for his sales pitch. "Why don't I leave a few samples of our new product here? I'll come back again when you're ready."

Pearl didn't say a word, just sniffled assent.

"She'll call you," Buzz said. He went to the counter and helped Everett return the supplies to his storage case.

With everything packed, Everett practically skipped out the door. I felt another low rumble from Max as Everett passed by. If not for his excellent manners, Max would probably have taken a nip out of his calf.

Buzz went to the other side of the counter and put an arm around Pearl. "I'm sorry, hon. Everett's right, though. Maybe it would help to focus on the business to keep your mind off what happened to Violet."

Pearl nodded, picked up the samples Everett had left, and headed to the back room.

"That was rough," Buzz said when Pearl was out of earshot. "She's built this business up, and to have that happen is a serious blow. But we've got to go one step at a time. Hopefully, the pet parade tomorrow will cheer her up. It's the biggest driver of her business for the year."

"There's certainly no love lost between Everett and Violet. Do you think he had anything to do with her death?"

Buzz stared solemnly into my eyes. "Frankly, I don't know. I don't want to think so," he said.

Max started scratching himself again. I hoped it wasn't a nervous habit he was developing. Maybe another massage was in his near future. He'd been through some stress over the last year. I reached down to quell the scratching so he didn't hurt himself.

"I'm looking forward to the parade. It's always a fun time. Mom and I will be there with the pups." Maybe some year I'd see if one of Joey's grandkids wanted to enter in the parade with one or both of the dogs. Might be a hoot.

"I've got to head to the store to pick up the ice cream supplies Wyatt and I are handing out to the kids at the end of the parade." Buzz was at the door, ready to leave.

"I've heard a lot about Wyatt. I hope to meet him tomorrow. Let's go, Max." I attached his leash, grabbed my bag of supplies, and we followed Buzz out the door. I still had no more answers to the question of who killed Violet.

CHAPTER FIVE

The pet parade tradition had been going on almost eighty years in this small town. Every August, kids and their pets would dress up and head down Main Street. The only purpose was fun. When I lived here, we always watched the parade but never had pets. I was envious of the other kids who had dogs and now I had my very own. Max and I headed to Caroline's to pick up some coffee and treats, and then we were picking up Mom and Trixie. If I decided to stay in town, maybe Max could partner up with one of Joey's grandkids next year to enter the contest. I pulled into the parking lot and we headed inside. Max veered to the display table where Caroline had several boxes of her signature gingersnap cookies for sale. Today was almost as big of a business boon for her as it was for Pearl. I tightened the leash to keep Max by my side. His sweet tooth ruled him again.

He stopped in his tracks and looked at me over his shoulder, his eyes pleading. *Maybe later, buddy.*

Caroline was busy behind the counter serving two other customers. Max and I waited our turn. "Hi, Chloe. What can I get you two?" Caroline chuckled. She'd started keeping a small jar of dog friendly ginger treats behind the counter for our visits. She handed me one and I fed it to Max. He carefully chewed it with his good manners. He gulped and smiled big, waiting for another one.

"You're spoiling him. I'm going to get a couple of coffees and a box of your mixed pastries, to go." When Caroline's pastries were fresh, they were mouth-watering. "Mom and I are taking the pups to the pet parade later."

Drool dripped from the left side of Max's mouth. He sat next to me, every part of his body still, except his stubby tail. He was in a staring contest with Caroline, begging for another treat. "Max," I said. He didn't budge, one mission on his mind. I laughed. His persistence paid off. "OK, Caroline, one more treat, then we have to cut him off." Fat chance. He always got what he wanted. She came around the counter and put the treat on the floor for him, then gave him a scratch behind his ears.

"You'll have to look for my float in the parade. It took a lot of work, but it's so cute. It's a giant slice of cake. It's set up so that it covers a wagon. My great-niece is going to pull it. She'll also have her dog that will be dressed as a cupcake."

"That sounds adorable." Max whimpered. We ignored him and he raised his voice.

"That's it for today, little buddy. He smells good," Caroline said.

"I know. It's those huckleberry products I got from Pearl's. I think she used the scrub when he was there the other day. I picked up some shampoo too."

Caroline returned behind the counter and washed her hands. She loaded the six pastries into a box. "I couldn't believe when I heard Violet was killed. And in Pearl's lobby. That's horrible." Caroline put two of the ginger treats into a bag and tucked them into the box. Max watched her the entire time, not missing a beat. He'd have to share one of those with Trixie when we got to Mom's.

"It is. Violet made some enemies, but who hated her enough to want to kill her?" I asked. "Buzz let me know that the Emerald Hills PD is not having much luck in the investigation."

Caroline placed the pastry box into a carrying bag and set it in front of me. Max took a step closer and placed his snout at the very edge of the counter, continuing to eyeball her. "Sadly, there were several people that she wasn't afraid to go against, no matter the consequences. Her protests against that proposed housing development got her a lot of notoriety. The Emerald Hills TV news crew even came and interviewed her."

"I know that project has definitely divided this town. Many are in favor of increasing the tax base and modernizing. But probably more people are opposed and want to maintain this slower, country pace of life," I said.

"She also filed that lawsuit against Everett," Caroline said. She got two paper coffee cups and lids and began to fill them.

"What was that about?" I asked.

"Apparently she thought his products had given Sasha a rash or discolored her snow-white fur or something," Caroline said. She placed the lids on the cups and put them into a carrier next to the bag.

I pulled out my credit card and paid for my purchases. "That sounds like Violet. Every time she took that dog to Pearl's, she argued with Joey about paying for the services. And I don't think Pearl ever got over the fact that Violet treated that purebred dog like a mutt."

Caroline got a tray of bear claws and loaded them into the display case.

I gathered my purchases and juggled them with Max's leash. "It seems Violet brought conflict with her wherever she went."

"Thankfully, I was never a part of that. I'll see you later at the parade," Caroline said.

I waved, and we headed out the door to Mom's. That housing development was definitely a big deal in this town. Probably the biggest deal since the gold rush. It would bring a lot of jobs for a while and grow the town in ways that would forever change the landscape. Many people's livelihoods were on the line with it. It would only be good for the Treehouse Hotel. We could always use more business.

CHAPTER SIX

"**M**om, why don't you get the dogs and I'll carry the chairs?"

We'd parked at Pearl's so we could position ourselves center street for the best vantage point for the parade. I leashed up the dogs and grabbed our chairs out of the back of the car. I heard lots of happy voices that sounded like the kids and their pets were ready for the show.

This would be a nice break from the hotel for a bit. Mom and I had been putting in a ton of work, and the units had started to look pretty great. Time with Mom, now that I'd moved from her house into the Buttercup Bungalow, was also much more pleasant. Max and I had our own space—and a much needed respite. Now that Mom had adopted Trixie, Max had gotten a break from that little stinker. She and Mom had become fast friends. For that, I was grateful.

The parking lots filled fast for what was sure to be a whole town event. We wove our way through the maze of cars. In a back window, I spotted one of the signs Violet used for her protests when demonstrating against the development. I wondered whose car it was. As far as I knew, Violet was the only one who stood out there at the park with her signs. We arrived at the front of Pearl's and I set up our chairs on the sidewalk.

More parade watchers lined the streets. I loved that this little town did something as quirky as a parade for their kids and dogs. The larger neighboring towns even began to participate. It turned out to be a pretty big moneymaker for a lot of businesses. Mom and I took our seats and waited for the show to start. The pups dutifully laid down next to us.

"Mom, I'm having dinner with Joey tonight."

Her head snapped toward me. "Find out about that Wyatt guy. I hope things are progressing nicely for them."

I was pretty sure Mom would have made a great detective. She was incredibly curious about most everything.

I checked my watch. Crowds of people continued to fill in. It was getting close to starting time.

Buzz and Pearl arrived to claim the two empty chairs next to us. "Hey, you two," Buzz said. Max and Trixie scrambled to attention. Buzz chuckled. "OK, I meant Chloe and Mabel. But I guess I'll greet you both as well." He bent over and gave some hefty back scratches, to the pups' utter delight.

"I can't wait for you to see the float this year for my business," Pearl said. "I've been working too hard on it. I'm sorry I had to be so secretive the other day at my shop. I just wasn't ready to spill the beans."

This parade meant a lot of customers for Pearl, and she committed a lot of time to it every year. One year she had a fully decked-out *Wizard of Oz* replication.

Buzz's chuckles continued. "You should see our garage. It looks like a construction zone with glitter, crepe paper, and streamers everywhere. Hey, there's Wyatt. I'll be right back. We're both handing out the ice cream to the kids at the end of the parade."

Just as soon as Buzz left, Judy arrived, strutting as if she was the queen of the world, the town her fiefdom. Her whole demeanor now that Violet was gone had become even more pompous, if that were possible. "Hello," Judy greeted with a formal parade wave. "This year is going to be the best yet." Max stood and looked at me, then looked at Judy. He looked back at me and approached Judy. She took a step back. "Get him off of me," she squealed. "Ugh, we have too many dogs in this parade. I'm so glad Violet's not in charge now. We need to have more cats. They're such better pets."

Max slightly lifted his right rear paw off the ground and looked at me with his peripheral vision.

I gave a shake of my head. That's all we needed. I patted my thigh.

He lowered his leg and sat, still on guard.

"Well, I have to go mingle. I am on the town council, after all. People expect me to be socializing," Judy said and darted away.

She continued down the sidewalk and met up with Buzz and Wyatt in front of the window next to Pearl's. Right behind her in big bold lettering was a sign that said Diamond Hills Development Company. How could I have not noticed that before? That must've been where Wyatt worked.

Mom leaned over and in a loud whisper said, "I really don't like her." Mom's directness was one quality I could use more of. She didn't waste time mincing words.

Max stood, barked, and wagged his tail, concurring. Judy really couldn't have been less sympathetic to Violet's death. I didn't expect her to be bawling, but at least show some compassion. Especially as a public figure, fake it, if nothing else. Did she have something to do with getting Violet out of the picture? It couldn't have been a better scenario for her.

"It looks like it's about to start," Mom said and started clapping.

I peered down the street and saw a 1959 fire-engine red convertible Corvette with Judy's husband Otis perched on top of the back seat. Flags whipped in the breeze from the side mirrors. Horns honked to signal the start of the show.

Buzz returned to his seat as we waited for the floats to arrive. Mom leaned over to him and in her loud whisper said, "Did Wyatt mention Joey?"

Buzz looked over Mom's head at me. I shrugged. "Um, no. Why would he?"

Mom sat back in her chair. "You know they're dating. They'll probably get married." She had already advanced the relationship several months or years down the road. I knew she only wanted the best for her kids. But this was pushing it. I would find out at dinner tonight just exactly how far this had gone. The last I'd heard, Wyatt had been dating Violet before she died. I just hoped he wasn't playing Joey for a fool.

Judy had roosted next to Otis in the lead car. She took it all in, obviously campaigning for mayor. Her stint on the city council had given her a platform to advance her political desires. She let no one or nothing stand in her way. Behind the lead car, the first float appeared with a little girl dressed in a Wonder Woman costume. She had a yellow Labrador retriever, grinning ear-to-ear, dressed in a Superman costume. And a black Labrador retriever dressed in a Darth Vader costume. The pets got just as big of a kick out of this as the kids, by the happy looks on their faces.

"My float's coming next," Pearl said. She clapped. "Look how good it turned out."

It was darned cute. Mom and I joined the clapping. Max stood up and lifted a paw toward Pearl's float. The front of the platform had a garbage can with a little girl, and a dog dressed in green, both peeking their heads out. The sign in front said *Sesame Street*. The back of the float had faux brick walls where Elmo and Cookie Monster were mounted. The commitment to these projects was serious. Next up, a wagon carried five pugs, each wrapped in a different-colored sweater with an M&M's label on their side. This parade was the highlight of my visit. Max turned and looked at me, wanting to join the fun. *I don't know, boy. I'm not sure we'll be here next year.* In the meantime, we were pretty busy fixing up the treehouses and solving the puzzle of Violet's death.

CHAPTER SEVEN

The din of the Smokehouse Restaurant made it hard to hear each other. Joey and I had gotten together a couple of times since I'd returned to town. I really enjoyed reconnecting with my sister. She always had a lot going on with her family. I was happy I could give her a breather once in a while. The place was hopping with the talk of the pet parade we had seen earlier that day. The joy of the kids and pets warmed the heart of even the most callous person.

"This is nice, getting some one-on-one time with my big sis," Joey said. For the longest time, I hated that reference. I was only the oldest by a few minutes of us triplets and somehow that put me in charge of the kids at home when Mom had to work. Now, I was happy to own it and help out in any way I could.

"It's crazy busy in here. We could have come another time so you could have worked and earned the tips."

Joey smiled warmly. "Nah, this is way better than any money. Wasn't that parade adorable? It gets better every year. It's one of the reasons I love this place."

I sipped my coffee. "Each float was cuter than the last. I might even enter Max and Trixie next year." I took another sip of my coffee.

"What? Does that mean you've decided to move back?" Joey almost squealed and bounced in her seat.

We placed the menus on the end of our table to signal to the waitress we were ready to order. "I'm seriously thinking about it. Now that I've moved from Mom's to the hotel, it's given me the separation to keep my sanity."

Joey gave a little finger wiggle to someone entering the restaurant. I looked out the corner of my eye to see Wyatt come through the door. He smiled big at her. I looked back at Joey, sure she blushed. She bowed her head and busied her hands with the napkin. "I would love it so much if you moved back. I don't get to see Zoe much, and I could really use a sister more prominently in my life." She kept her head down.

I had a giant grin on my face. It was clear that there was a spark between Joey and Wyatt. "I agree. And working on fixing up the hotel with Mom has been a blessing for me too. It's bringing back good memories of the projects Frank and I did together before he passed. I loved admiring the results when we had finished."

Joey lifted her head. She giggled, while continuing to fidget with the napkin. The waitress came and took our orders, giving Joey a reprieve from my quizzing. I took another sip of my coffee and slowly set the cup down. I folded my hands on the table.

"OK, so yes, I like Wyatt. There, I said it."

I held up my hand. "It's none of my business. But, how did you two meet?"

Joey snuck a peak at Wyatt across the room. Her pink cheeks returned. "His office is next to Pearl's. I was out on a walk one day and we almost literally ran into each other when I rounded the corner."

"You know," I started. "Mom already has you two married."

She sat back, a serious look on her face. "Chloe, I really have learned my lesson. If anything is going to happen, I'm taking it slow. If I marry again, it has to be for a final time. I have to be done with all the drama."

I saw movement again near Wyatt's table. Judy had entered the restaurant and joined him in the booth. "Well, that seems odd," I said.

Joey followed my gaze.

"Why would Judy be having dinner with Wyatt?" I continued.

Joey shrugged. "Probably something to do with that development he's working on. He's always so busy with it that he doesn't have time for much else."

The waitress arrived with our meals. We placed our napkins on our laps and dug in. The restaurant really honed their smoked meat process. Everything was mouthwatering. "He's probably not shedding a tear with Violet's departure. I bet she made a lot of trouble for him," I said.

Joey continued her solemn tone. "You don't know the half of it. Every time Violet marched at the property with her protest sign, another investor seemed to disappear. Wyatt was livid last week when the largest one pulled out."

I devoured my barbecued chicken dinner. I would have to get some take-out and keep a stash of this at home. Maybe even a morsel or two for Max. "She certainly wasn't shy about her views. When a couple of the newest treehouses were being built at the hotel, she chained herself to the trees, claiming they were crying and she had to save them," I said.

Joey slyly grabbed another peek at Wyatt. That girl was smitten. I was happy for her. If he treated her well, then they should be together.

"I couldn't stand her either," Joey said. "Every time she came into Pearl's I wanted to leave. About half the time, she had me in tears. I tried everything I could to avoid her."

Max and I had started our list of suspects for Violet's murder. Reluctantly, I had to put my sister there, as she was present when Violet died. Even as mad as Violet made her, I couldn't see her harming a hair on anyone's head.

"Does Wyatt have enough investors for the development to go forward?" I asked. The waitress arrived to refill my coffee and I waved her away. I would be up all night if I didn't quit now.

Joey sat her napkin on the table and pushed her plate back. "He had a couple of people that wanted to, but he wasn't sure their financing would come through. The last time Everett came to Pearl's to stock us up on products, he bragged how he was going to invest. He really wanted to be a bigwig and get out of hawking pet supplies. He was so mad when Violet kept badmouthing his huckleberry scrub. That had been his bestseller until she filed that stupid lawsuit for damages to her dog."

"Wow, it must have been bad," I said.

She shook her head. "Not really. When Violet brought Sasha in it looked like she had one scratch she'd given herself. There was no evidence it was because of Everett's products. But Violet insisted it was. Even if it wasn't, the damage to Everett's reputation, and his finances, was done. That only amped up her smug attitude. She felt like she always had to fight for the underdog, even if it meant making enemies."

The waitress placed our bill on the table. I agreed with Joey. Sister time was long overdue. Living so far away, I had missed a lot of family get togethers. Was this worth the move back to town? "This was wonderful. Thank you." I packed up my doggie bag with treats for my boy. I couldn't wait to bring him home a surprise and snuggle in for a puzzle, but my head throbbed trying to piece together the mystery of Violet's murder. I needed me some Max time so we could sort it all out.

CHAPTER EIGHT

The brightness of the yellow decor played well off the brown wood from the tree and treehouse. Buttercup Bungalow was one of my favorite units because of the prominence of the trees inside the building. One branch of the tree was situated to be used as a bench in the corner by a window. It made an amazing reading nook, the perfect place to peer out at the territorial views. Getting Mom up the stairs to this unit was also easier than most of the others. I was glad I decided to help with renovations so she didn't have to chance hurting herself scaling the entrances. I carried our decorating supplies up the steps and returned to the bottom to retrieve Mom. Max scurried behind me, supervising each part of the journey.

I took Mom's arm to support her climbing the steps. "I've got everything upstairs, Mom."

She pulled her arm away. "I can do it, Chloe." And she marched right up to the door without missing a beat. I stayed close behind, in case I needed to catch her. I hoped I was as spry and spunky as she was at her age. Somehow she managed to keep her wits about her and she was pretty good at getting around. I had definitely inherited her independence.

Max and I entered the door and scanned our project, assessing where to start. I had enough decorations for a room twice this size. "Mom, feel free to take a seat and point to where you'd like us to put the items."

She took me up on my offer and plopped down onto the tree trunk. "We really need a cushion for this thing," she said and patted it. "First, why don't you put the rug next to the bed. That way someone will have something warm on their feet when they get up."

I got the oval yellow and gray rug out of the bag and placed it parallel with the bed. Right on cue, Max settled onto it, christening it approved. He stood and started furiously scratching again. I wondered if that huckleberry shampoo was drying out his skin. I'd need to check with Pearl and see what else she had that might help.

"Did you bathe him? Why is he always scratching?" Mom asked. She got up and retrieved the yellow curtains from another shopping bag.

I looked at my boy. He shrugged. "I just did. Maybe it's the dry air," I suggested.

Max stood and went into the bathroom. What could he be doing? His bed and food were in the main living area. As I got to the bathroom he met me at the door with a piece of paper in his mouth. I should have known. I pulled it from him, expecting it to be a receipt from my decorating purchases. Instead, I found a label from the huckleberry shampoo. Why would he do that?

I peered over his shoulder and saw all of the labels from all of the dog supplies lying on the floor. What in the world? As I got closer, I saw all of the bottles still had labels, but different ones. I picked up one and looked at the back. The ingredients were definitely chemicals and not at all the natural, organic variety the other label advertised. These were the products I bought from Pearl the first time I took him to her pet spa. As far as I knew, Everett was the only supplier for these products in town, which meant one thing—Everett was scamming Pearl.

"Way to go, Max," I said.

Mom joined us in the bathroom doorway. "What did he do now?" she asked. "Oh, boy. Did he rip those labels off? I knew he ate paper. You really should keep a better eye on him."

Except Max had just discovered a piece to the puzzle of what may have been a motive for Violet's death. If she discovered Everett had been deceiving people with inferior products, her lawsuit against him was justified. I needed to get to Pearl's and find out what she knew about this. It might be news to her.

"Let's keep going here, Mom. We need to finish this so we can start on the Morning Glory Manor."

She returned to her perch.

Max looked at me and grinned. His tail wagged, showing his pleasure that he'd discovered another clue.

"So tell me what happened with Joey last night?" Mom prepared for a gossip recap.

I pulled the two lemon-colored lamps out of another bag. The base was almost shaped like the fruit and the shades had a diamond pattern of yellow and gray. The lights would also brighten up the natural darkness of the interior.

"We had a nice time. I realized how much I missed my sisters." Max got up and circled the rug. He eyed me, knowing what was coming next.

"That's why you should move back, Chloe. Just make your mind up finally and do it." Max approached me as I held a lamp in each hand. He nodded his head yes, in approval of Mom's plan. I think he'd finally gotten used to Trixie and would probably miss her if we left. And the major league puzzle we had to solve kept us busy. It didn't hurt that he got to live in a tree. What dog wouldn't love that?

"I'm still thinking about it. There's a lot to consider."

Mom gazed out the window.

"Wyatt was at the restaurant too."

Mom jerked her head back to my direction. "Did you guys talk to him?"

I continued to retrieve our treasures from the bags and place them around the room. With each one, the place smiled a little brighter. "No. Actually, he was having dinner with Judy."

Mom stood and went to the night table to straighten a lamp. "What? Oh, maybe they were talking about his new development. That's all she can talk about. Like it's going to be her legacy or something."

I gathered up the empty bags and sat on the bed. "It's probably the biggest thing to happen in this town since the treehouses were built."

"It'll be interesting to see if it goes through, even after Violet's death. Her legacy was trying to preserve the natural beauty. We definitely have that with the treehouses. But a housing development? That's just too big-city for us," Mom said.

I looked at her, uncertain what her response to my idea would be. Ever since I had arrived to help her restore this place, I'd been thinking about what we could do to really secure the future business. "So, Mom. I want to pass something by you that I've been thinking about. Something that could really launch this place back into prosperity."

She tilted her head toward me. Max stood and mimicked her, ready for my brainstorm.

I gulped. "I'm thinking if we added a lodge and maybe a couple more units, we could really grow the business. The lodge could be a gathering place for a lot of events in town and we could advertise for out-of-town guests to have their meetings or events here."

Mom got up and circled the little room. She returned to the bench. "Hmm."

Seriously, that's all I got? "What do you think?"

Max barked three times. I took that as a yes from him.

Mom looked at Max. "I agree with him. It's a great idea, Chloe. I love it!"

I'd never gotten that resounding of an endorsement from Mom for any of my ideas. I got up and hugged her. Max joined in and leaned against our legs.

"OK. Let me call the permit office and see what we need to do." This would no doubt take some time. But it would keep me really busy here until I finished my work on the place.

CHAPTER NINE

M ax and I wove our way through the variety of displays Caroline had in her store. The business seemed to be picking up, but she continued selling just about anything and everything that had nothing to do with coffee or pastries. Max beelined to the counter, ready for his treat. Caroline spoiled him at every visit with his favorite gingersnaps.

"Hey, two of my favorite customers," Caroline greeted. She wiped her hands on her apron and opened the dog treat jar.

Max politely placed a paw on the edge of the counter. Caroline retrieved his snack and placed it right next to him. He scooped it onto the floor and quickly nibbled it up. He expectantly returned his paw to the counter.

I laughed. "Never hurts to ask, right?" I rubbed Max's head. He looked at me over his shoulder, persistent in his quest. "Maybe later, boy. After our walk." He gently and obediently pulled his paw down. "Coffee, a bear claw and, of course, a couple of treats for my boy."

Caroline got one of the pastries from the display case and placed it in a bag. "Where are you going on your walk?" she asked.

Max slowly wandered to the other side of the hat rack. I suspected he was trying another angle to convince Caroline of just one more treat. If that was the case, I'd reward him for his ingenuity.

"Cedarbrook Trails. We haven't had much time to visit and I could use a change of scenery. Although, it's not much different than the treehouse landscape."

Caroline poured my coffee, put the lid on, and handed it to me. "It really is beautiful there. I'm so torn between keeping that pristine natural place or the housing development. One reason I live here is the peaceful nature. But that development would be great for my business and the town coffers."

Max was now nowhere in sight. I expected him to emerge on the other side of the counter right next to Caroline. That boy was clever.

"I agree. It's given me some ideas about how to improve the business at the hotel. I really want to set Mom up well by the time I'm finished renovating. If my plans pan out, we'll really have a great family asset on our hands." I stood on my tiptoes to see if Max had made it around the counter. "Do you see my boy over there?"

Caroline looked to her left and shook her head no. OK, he'd wandered off to who knew where? Probably trying to get someone else to share their treats. I went to the end of the counter near the hat rack. A familiar voice wafted through the display. I didn't see Judy when we came in. She was seated alone at a small table tucked into a corner. She must have been on the phone.

"Don't worry. With Violet out of the way, you and I are totally in the clear." Her head tilted toward the window with her right hand held to her ear.

Max approached Judy's table with stealth moves. With her head in her papers she didn't see him. I spotted his prey. A plate full of gingersnaps right in front of Judy. I clicked my tongue to get his attention. He took two more steps in Judy's direction. She continued in her oblivion to her surroundings.

"Wyatt, trust me. With the two of us together, there's no stopping us," Judy said.

I couldn't believe my ears. Judy and Wyatt were having an affair. They didn't even try to hide it at the restaurant last night. Joey would be crushed. But if he was a scoundrel, better to find out now. I didn't want to be the one to tell her. She had such a sparkle in her eye last night that I hadn't seen in a long time.

Max's head almost touched the plate with Judy's cookies on it. She turned, and seeing him for the first time, jumped back. "Get away, you mutt," she yelled. She slammed her phone down and shooed him with her hands. "Go away! How rude!"

Max growled. He shook his head from side to side. "Sorry about that. He's usually so polite to everyone he meets. Come here, Max," I said. He stood his ground and raised a paw. He tapped Judy's leg.

She squealed and scooted her chair further into the corner. "He's attacking me. Get that vicious animal away from here."

I took hold of Max's collar. "I'm pretty sure he's just after your cookies," I said. I tried to pull him toward me. He refused. He pawed at her leg again. I smiled.

Judy moved her plate out of Max's reach. "It's not funny. He could really hurt someone," she said.

Max, confident his message was received, obediently sat by my side. "That must be cat hair on your pants. I think he's just smelling the fur."

Judy looked down and swiped her pant leg. "I don't see anything. And that's why I have cats. They would never be so aggressive toward me and steal food off my plate." Judy had at least five cats, probably more by now. They were more unruly than Max could ever be. Judy had promised her cats would be entered into next year's pet parade now that Violet's "no cats" rule was null and void. It would be a three-ring circus.

"We're headed out anyway," I said. Max relented and let me lead him away from the table. His stealth hearing was another tool in our puzzle-solving box. "We're going to explore the Cedarbrook Trails. I haven't been there since I came back. I'm sure it's changed a lot."

Judy scoffed and waved us away. "Enjoy it while you can."

Max whimpered. *Yes, buddy. We have to compare notes. I can't tell who's coming and going in this mystery of Violet's death.* Exploring the trails would help us clear the fog in our brains to figure out what was really going on. I grabbed my purchase from the counter and waved goodbye to Caroline. Max whimpered again. "I'm as surprised as you are, Max. I never would have pegged Judy to be having an affair with Wyatt. Otis is going to be devastated. And once they've been found out, her stint on the city council will surely come to an end, her reign over this little town finished. Let's go."

CHAPTER TEN

M ax perched on the passenger seat of my car, navigating us to one of the trailheads at Cedarbrook Trails. We couldn't wait to explore the ten miles. Although today, maybe we'd just do a short stint to warm us up for a longer one at a later date. I parked, and we got out of the car. I took a deep breath to inhale the fresh, clean air. "Ah, some much needed clearing, Max." He wagged in agreement.

The signs offered multiple paths for every desire. We didn't have much time today, so we chose the shorter Cherry Hills loop. I leashed him up and we headed down the path. This place was a haven for outdoor lovers and had something for just about everybody, whether you were on a horse, a bike, or just your own feet. Thankfully, it was still cool enough and there was plenty of shade to rest when needed. The fir and pine forests spanned as far as your eye could see.

We began our ascent to the first hill. It was a gradual incline, but I started to breathe a little heavier. Max trotted along as if this were a total breeze for him. I needed to get into better shape so this wouldn't be our last trip. We reached the peak and I bent over to catch my breath. After about thirty seconds I took a seat on a bench to take in the view. The Emerald Hills valley in the distance teemed with wildflowers of every color. This time of year was primetime to enjoy so much in bloom. However, the fall colors rivaled this show when the leaves began to turn. Even the snow in winter provided a wonderland of beauty. I was pretty sure Max would adjust plenty well to a move here. But could I?

My life had been my own for several decades. Before my husband Frank passed, it was just the two of us. We played hard and adventured every moment we had. A return to this town meant a whole new era in my life, one I needed to prepare for.

"Alright, boy, let's keep going." I stood and Max sped ahead. We ventured down the other side of the first hill. The view changed to be the forest floor. Less light permeated the treetops. The foliage and underbrush thickened on both sides of us. I was thankful the trails were well-worn so we wouldn't get lost.

A *clop-clop* noise came from the opposite direction. I briefly stopped to confirm the sound wasn't just my fast-beating heart. I wasn't sure how Max would react to seeing a horse. He began to prance as he spotted the large animal, raising his knees in rhythm with the horse's clopping. I strained the leash to slow him down. We moved to a wide spot on the side of the trail where we could wait for them to pass. Max obediently sat to watch the parade. The horse and rider slowed a bit as they went by, waving.

I returned the wave and Max lifted his front leg, offering a greeting. Could he get any cuter? The more we were together, the more I noticed his genius and engaging personality. Cats schmats. Judy didn't know what she was missing by not having a dog. I waited until the distraction had sufficiently disappeared. Max and I returned to the trail. I began walking and he wouldn't budge. I gave a little tug and he leaned back, more solidly attached to the ground.

"What is it, Max?" I bent over and examined his legs. Was he injured? Or had he come into contact with poison oak? I had a small first-aid kit in my backpack. I hoped it wasn't something worse. I gently cradled each leg and felt for an injury. Nothing appeared wrong.

He stood up, turned ninety degrees to the right, and sat back down. What? Was I getting the silent treatment for some reason? I moved and stood in front of him. I crouched down and gave him the once-over again. Had I missed something the first time? "I don't get it, Max." I stood up and peered down at him with my hands on my hips. He craned his neck around my left leg. I turned around and saw them. Large red spray-painted Xs marked several of the trees about ten yards off the path. I knew what that meant. Someone had already been here to identify which trees were coming down to make room for the development. I had no idea it was this far along. I was actually skeptical that it would go forward. This town wasn't one to adapt to a lot of changes, especially one as big as the housing project. There were a lot of hoops to jump through, albeit less now that Violet was gone.

"Looks like we may have found another piece to the puzzle. Let's keep going to see where this leads us," I said.

Max pranced again, much more buoyed than I felt. We continued for about a hundred yards to another wide spot in the trail. I carefully led Max through the brush to avoid any danger.

The farther we went from the main trail, the more red Xs we discovered. I stopped and shook my head. But I couldn't deny what was right in front of us. We returned to the trail. A sign told us we were halfway through the Cherry Hills loop. We continued on for the second half of our trip. We wound through a mix of open and dense areas as we approached the edge of the Cedarbrook Trails property.

If my internal navigation was accurate, we should be near the hotel property. We searched for an opening to again venture off the main trail. My heart sank. I saw Buttercup Bungalow in the distance. I was sure this was the hotel property. I counted over twenty trees marked to be taken down. Max approached the nearest one and lifted his leg, expressing both of our displeasures for what we had discovered. How could Mom or I not have known this was happening? This development was enormous. It would more than triple the size of this small town. No wonder Wyatt was trying to get more investors. Making this happen was going to cost a pretty penny. And that was just for the building expenses. The inevitable lawsuits would rival that bill. With that kind of money on the line, people could do unspeakable things. If Violet saw what was happening, she would be turning in her grave.

"Max, we have to find out what's going on. My dream for expanding the treehouses might just have been dashed. I hope it's not too late." Max jumped on me and slurped my cheek, ready to take on our foe.

"With her town council position, Judy's the only one who could have pushed this through so quickly without us knowing about it." Max growled. His eyebrows angled down and his jowls dipped. One mention of Judy changed his whole demeanor. "Let's go, boy." We jogged the remainder of the way to our car, re-energized for our mission.

CHAPTER ELEVEN

I was steamed that I hadn't put the clues together earlier about Judy's plans. She was a person who always had to have top-of-the-line things in her life. Nothing wrong with wanting the best, but to scheme your way to it was another story. According to Joey, she found Judy standing over Violet's body when she discovered them in the lobby at Pearl's. Judy's personality made you bristle, but was she devilish enough to want Violet dead? Would Violet's threats to tie up the development for years in court for environmental issues cause Judy to snap? I placed my hand on Max's back as he sat in the copilot seat of the car. The warmth of his body and his steady pulse calmed me. He looked at me, his eyes concerned for my well-being. "Thanks, boy." His stubby tail thumped.

We pulled into Pearl's parking lot. I reached in back, grabbed my purse and the bag with the jar labels that Max had found. Max and I were becoming frequent visitors at Pearl's. My boy deserved every pampering treatment they had. So far he'd had a massage and a bath with the huckleberry scrub. When we solved Violet's murder he would be treated to the rejuvenation package, including the Moroccan oil rub down and Dead Sea salts scrub.

We entered the lobby where the familiar bell jingled. Joey was the cashier today, another nice surprise. She and Pearl had their heads together. Joey gave a wave and a huge smile when she saw us. Max ran toward her as she crouched for a big hug. "Hey buddy, we don't have you down for an appointment. To what do we owe this surprise visit?" she asked.

From behind the counter, Sasha, Violet's poodle emerged. "Oh, Sasha's here," I said.

Pearl approached her and stroked her thick fur. It looked exceptionally nice, probably an extra special cut from Pearl. She had never liked how Violet treated Sasha. With her pedigree, that dog could have regularly placed very well at national dog shows. "I'm taking care of her for now. She can finally be treated in the manner she should have been all along." Pearl hugged Sasha and closed her eyes.

Sasha greeted me. Her fur was as soft as newborn baby hair. The poodle curls looked as if they'd been individually styled. She had a large pink bow clipped to the back of her neck. "She looks great," I said.

"Did you guys need some more supplies already?" Pearl asked.

I looked at Max. He came to my side. "No, I have something I wanted to share with you. I hope it's not a surprise. But I'm afraid it will be." I took the bag of labels and dumped the contents onto the counter.

Pearl looked at me. She frowned and shook her head. "What is this?" she asked.

I straightened out of a few of the labels. "For the last couple of days, Max has been scratching more than normal. I thought maybe his skin was dry, so I applied some of the moisturizer. But it seemed to get worse."

Pearl picked up each label, examined them, and lined them up on the counter. She shook her head again. "What's this? Everett has been scamming me. Not just me, but all my customers." Pearl's shoulders droop with frustrated defeat. "Chloe, I can't believe this is happening to me. After everything else I've been through."

I continued. "I went into the bathroom and saw all of the labels for every product I bought from Everett had fallen off the bottles and were on the floor. Underneath each one was another label. I looked closer and saw the ingredients on the labels still on the bottles were mostly chemicals. I think Everett relabeled these so he could charge more."

Pearl ambled over and plopped into one of the waiting chairs. Max approached and rested his chin on her knee. His brown eyes radiated love. She rubbed his head. "I'm so sorry, Max. How could I have missed this?" Pearl's voice cracked. She treated every customer as a part of her family and the dogs like they were her own kids.

I shoved all the labels back into the bag. "I'm sorry, Pearl," I said.

Pearl stood, her fists balled, her back straightened. "I knew he always wanted more than this pet supply business. But to do that to defense-less animals for his own gain? That's so wrong." She grabbed the bag from me, crumpled it up, and barged through the door to the back room.

I took a seat in one of the guest chairs. Max joined me in the adjoining seat to my right. "After everything she's been through, I hated to have to tell her that." I put my arm around Max and he leaned into me. "Until we can solve the mystery of Violet's death, her business will keep suffering."

Joey joined us in the waiting area, sitting in the chair to Max's right. Her eyes were red and puffy. "Are you OK?" I was so intently focused on those labels I missed how upset she was.

She turned away. "Yes."

"Joey, what's going on?" I reached past Max and placed my hand on her shoulder. Max put his paw on top of my hand.

Joey chuckled. "You'd think working in a dog spa that I'd have a dog by now. But my kids and grandkids keep me busy enough." She tipped her chin down. "I don't want to be a burden."

I waited.

"Brady was arrested for stealing," was all she could get out before losing it. She bent over. "He tried so hard. I thought it was getting better. With his priors, this won't be good." Joey's oldest son had been a troublemaker from day one. Not major stuff, usually nothing to harm people. But vandalism, petty theft. He'd been taken on as an apprentice at the local mechanic shop.

"I'm so sorry, hon. What happened?" I got up, faced her, crouched down, and held her hands. Max stood and hugged her with both of his front legs.

"I don't know exactly. When Violet was last in here, she accused him of stealing something from her. She had hired him to do some yard work. He claimed he didn't take whatever she said he did."

I retrieved a handful of tissues from the counter and pressed them into Joey's hand.

She dabbed her eyes and nose. "The thing is, Chloe, I believe him this time. I don't know why. I just have a feeling."

I lifted Joey's chin to look into her eyes. "Trust your instinct. I mean, definitely find out the truth. But why would he mess up a good thing he had at Marv's Mechanical?"

Max made the quietest bark I'd ever heard from him. We both laughed. "And that's from someone who has great instincts. He knows," I said and stood up.

"You're both right. When I got the call, I was scared it was worse." Joey took all of the tissues and muffled her cries. Her family certainly put her through the ringer. "I mean, theft is bad. But what if Brady got mad at Violet for accusing him? What if he had something to do with her death?"

"Joey, trust that he didn't. From what Max and I have uncovered, he had nothing to do with it. Just take one step at a time."

She stood and wrapped her arms around me. The stakes for Max and me to solve this murder raised every day.

CHAPTER TWELVE

Max and I had a messy enough puzzle on our hands with Violet's death. I now also had to find out what was really going on with this housing development. At every turn, new information was revealed that indicated there was a lot of behind-the-scenes maneuvering. I couldn't let Mom find out that there were complications. She was so excited about the possible expansion of the hotel, already planning names for the two new treehouses. Could Wyatt prevent our future expansion? Or worse, cause us to tear down some of our existing units? I took a deep breath and entered the city hall building. I had to keep my focus neutral until I knew there was something to really be upset about.

The clerk behind the counter asked, "How can I help you?"

I stepped up to face her. "Is this where I find out about getting a building permit?"

"It sure is," the clerk continued. It said Theresa on her name tag. "What type of building are we talking about? And where?"

I set my thick file folder on the counter. In case I'd need to reference some prior hotel documents, I'd brought all that I could find. There was still a lot of bookkeeping to go through to get it all organized. I hoped everything I needed was in there.

"We're looking at expanding the Cedarbrook Treehouse Hotel by a couple of new units and adding a lodge," I said.

Theresa tilted her head and looked at me over the top of her glasses. "Are you Chloe?"

I stared at her, compelling my memory to kick into gear. "Yes, I am. My mom, Mabel, owns it. I'm in town to help her for now. I'm sorry. I haven't been here much lately. Do I know you?" With the size of this town, it wouldn't take me long to get reacquainted with every single resident.

She shook her head. "Nah, we haven't met. I'm friends with your niece, Brittany. She said you were back helping."

I smiled. It never hurt to make more friends in this town, especially ones that could help sort out the mess with the hotel. "When I called earlier, the person I talked to mentioned that there was a hold on any new permits for the hotel right now. Can you tell me why? I'm not aware of any issues."

"Sure, just a sec." Theresa left the front counter and went to a room that was filled floor to ceiling with filing cabinets. She pulled open a couple of drawers and inserted placeholders where she removed some large files. She lugged them out to the front counter and plopped the dust buckets down in front of me. "Sorry about that. Paper seems to be a magnet for dust. We try to keep the room aired out. It helps some." She thumbed through the piles of paper, taking several items out and placing them to the side. Satisfied she had found what she was looking for, she turned around a stack of papers to face me. "There's a couple of things. Right here, it looks like someone named Violet had filed an appeal against the approval of the original construction. It looks like that was resolved. But in the event expansion ever came up, she submitted another appeal to preempt anything from even being approved to start." Theresa pointed to a location on the paper with Violet's signature.

I took a step back and held my nose to prevent a sneeze. "Well, how do I get that removed so we can submit our proposal?" I lost the battle and sneezed three times. My eyes watered. I pulled a tissue from my purse to stifle the flow.

Theresa returned the first stack of papers to the folder and closed it. "That's the type of thing that has to go to the town council for review. They actually have a meeting later today. Agenda items have to be submitted a week in advance to be discussed. But you could speak during the public comment period if you want."

I held my nose to stifle any more sneezes or I'd never get through this conversation. "Is that all I have to do? Just show up? I don't have to get permission from anyone?"

"Nope, that's it," she said.

I smiled. That step seemed pretty simple. I'd make some notes beforehand so that I could succinctly make my pitch to proceed with our proposal. I was buoyed by that news. "You said there were a couple of things. What's the second one?" If it was as straightforward as the first, I'd soon have some good news for Mom.

Theresa held a second stack of papers close to her chest. "This one looks like a much bigger deal." She fanned out the paperwork in front of me.

I looked up at her for an explanation. "Can you help me understand this? I'm not sure what I'm looking at." I furrowed my brow and concentrated on the first piece of paper she pointed at.

"This one here is an application for that new housing development. This is the really big project that's going to change this town forever." She looked up at me slowly to see my response.

I still wasn't tracking her line of thought. "OK."

She pointed to a second piece of paper that showed approval to proceed with clearing land. Public land. The portion of the trees that Max had spotted at Cedarbrook Trails. And to clear the portion that overlapped onto the hotel property. Her finger slid over to the signature line where I read Judy Livingston. "The paperwork to begin the official development has been submitted and approved. This is on the council agenda today for them to give the final consent to start clearing the land."

I took a step back, stunned. With as little fanfare as humanly possible, this would do exactly as Theresa said. Change this town in ways that nobody could imagine or approve. And I bet it had happened right under everyone's nose. Judy wasn't having an affair with Wyatt. She was directly involved in shoving this development forward. She must be one of his investors. I couldn't let this happen. Even if I didn't get approval to expand the hotel, I had to stop this destruction. Violet's shenanigans and protests had been a constant burr in the saddle of the town council. But could her opposition to the development be the reason someone killed her?

CHAPTER THIRTEEN

A smattering of people filled the rows of chairs facing the dais. The town council meeting was scheduled to start in about fifteen minutes. I took a seat in the back row. I needed to observe the process before I stepped to the microphone and made the pitch of my life. Judy looked like she was holding court chatting with her fellow council members, throwing her head back laughing like she was in the catbird seat. I looked down at the notepad on my lap. I made notes of what I wanted to say when my time came to speak. I ticked through each point in my head. I had no idea what would happen after that. I hoped the decision wouldn't take long. That would put a huge damper on the hotel future and my planned stay in town. The audience chairs continued to fill as the clock ticked toward the top of the hour. The council members meandered to their seats as the mayor gaveled the meeting to order. He began with introductory comments to review the agenda topics for the day. Most of the council busied themselves with papers in front of them, heads down. The mayor announced the first agenda item.

"Today, we're going to name as Milly Kennedy day. We want to recognize Milly for her work with homeless kids." The mayor read a proclamation honoring Milly and her tireless efforts for the food and clothing drives. When he finished reading, he got up and descended to the podium in front of the dais. An elderly woman, who I assumed to be Milly, stood and met him in the front of the room. We all clapped as the mayor handed Milly a certificate, shook her hand, and they turned for a picture. Milly and her family filed out of the room. The mayor then returned to his seat. He shuffled papers and moved on to the next topic, the upcoming election for mayor.

"Since I'm stepping down as mayor at the end of my term, we'll soon have a new person filling this seat." He turned and looked at Judy. She sat tall, soaking it all in. "The original candidates on the ballot included Judy Livingston, Violet Connelly, and Anthony Warren. With Violet's untimely death, we're down to two people vying for the position. Judy shook her head yes. The smug look on her face assumed victory. *Well, we'll just see.*

The mayor continued, "Since we're so close to the election, we don't have time to alter the ballots to remove Violet's name. We will proceed as is."

"That's OK. Everyone knows she's gone," Judy butted in. All heads swiveled toward her. She slumped in her chair, appearing a bit embarrassed by her interruption.

With an audible sigh, the mayor continued to the next agenda item. "Next up we have our public comment period. We've also got a sizable topic at the end of our time today. We'll take a fifteen-minute break after our public comment time before we finish our meeting."

I gazed around to see if anyone else was going to speak. Immediately, a young man sprang up and approached the podium. He introduced himself and launched into a diatribe about the importance of the town's history. He insisted the council recognize and vote to change the name of the town after one of his distant relatives. He wanted it called Herbold's Burgh after Edward Herbold. Judy chuckled, which drew a dirty look from the mayor. She stifled her laugh and covered her mouth with her hand, still shaking her head no. If she was going to be mayor, she'd have to work on her poker face.

The mayor thanked the young man, who proudly returned to his seat. The mayor inquired if there were any other speakers for today's meeting. I rose from my seat and made a beeline to the front of the room. I placed my notes on the podium and stilled my shaking hands by holding its sides. I slowly panned my eyes to each of the council members, arriving lastly at Judy. Her smile turned upside down. Her jovial demeanor had disappeared.

"Thank you for the opportunity to comment. My name is Chloe Carson. My family owns the Cedarbrook Treehouse hotel." I placed my finger where I had left off in my notes. "I recently learned of an appeal that was previously submitted by Violet Connelly preventing any future development at the location." I paused and swallowed, preparing for a strong closing statement. "I respectfully request that appeal be denied." I cleared my throat, relaxed my shoulders, and dropped my arms to my side. I quickly glanced up from my notes. Most of the council rummaged through their paperwork, shifting papers left and right. I looked down and continued. "We plan to submit a proposal to expand the hotel by adding two additional units and a lodge. The units would be consistent with what we have now. The lodge would be designed to provide a venue for many of the larger events that currently have to be held in our neighboring city, Emerald Hills. Our town would have a place where we could gather, and by drawing business, help support the town budget. Thank you for your consideration." Talk money and everyone listened.

"Thank you for the comments, Chloe. I acknowledge Violet disrupted and damaged this town and our business future for a long time." Judy had jumped in ahead of the mayor's comments. She spoke as if she was giving a stump speech. "I appreciate you bringing this to our attention."

Was that it? Was I dismissed? "You're welcome." I waited.

The council began to talk amongst themselves while Judy and Councilman Ford guffawed.

"So what are the next steps?" I asked.

"Well," Judy began, further speaking over the mayor. "We take the matter under advisement. After we thoroughly analyze, we'll decide how to proceed." She turned back to Councilman Ford. They continued their laughter.

"Thank you, Chloe." The mayor quickly resumed his role. "As Judy said, we'll let you know if the appeal is removed. If it is, you're free to proceed with your proposal. Once the permit department receives that, we'll have another public comment period."

I straightened my notes and smiled. "Thank you, and if I may, I would also like to comment on the proposed development."

All talk stopped. Judy glared at me.

"Of course," said the mayor. "This is your time."

Judy continued her efforts at intimidation. She placed both hands on the surface in front of her and leaned forward. "What about it?"

I gulped and grabbed the podium again, prepared for an even more hostile response to my comments. "I have discovered the planned development includes the taking of property from the hotel. I want to let you know that I'm planning to submit an appeal to prevent that."

Judy grinned. "You can't do that. The development is claiming eminent domain. It's in the long-term interest of the town, more than your little treehouses are."

I straightened my papers and looked down. Did I have any chance to stop this? We would barely be able to keep enough units in operation, let alone expand, if this development went through. "I understand that. However, I don't believe the proper steps were followed, and I will still be submitting my paperwork," I said. I was hopeful but not optimistic. With Judy ruling the roost, anything could happen.

"We'll now take a fifteen-minute break before our last topic this meeting. All adjourned until then." The mayor slammed the gavel down. Judy and Councilman Ford had their heads together, an intense conversation happening. I had no idea if my comments would make a difference, but I had to try.

I turned and headed down the aisle toward the exit for a breather until the council resumed after the break. What would I tell Mom?

If that appeal wasn't lifted, that would be a huge blow to the future of the hotel. Or worse. If that development took over hotel property, that might ultimately be the end of the legacy. Just as I pushed open the council room door, a hand pulled it from the other side. Standing right in front of me was Wyatt.

CHAPTER FOURTEEN

"Hi, Chloe." Wyatt held the door for me to leave. I didn't move. After an awkward pause, he stepped around me and continued into the meeting room. I turned around to see him sit in the front row. Judy gave him a friendly wave. He nodded his head. Wyatt set a paper roll and his large briefcase on the chair next to him and clicked the latches open. I returned to my seat in the back row for this portion of the program. It was about to get interesting. Although this was a public meeting, most people never had any idea of the significant business done by government that affected their lives, all done in plain sight. Wyatt retrieved a large file folder and snapped his briefcase shut. The mayor looked at the clock and signaled the rest of the council to return to their seats. Time felt like it stood still as the mayor opened the second part of the meeting.

"Our last agenda topic for this meeting is final approval of the proposed Diamond Hills housing development. I'm going to read into the record the specifics of the project. Then we will do a review of the plans and wrap up with a review of the financial details." The mayor described the specifics of what had been requested. The four hundred and twenty acres to be developed, the combination of mixed use and housing, the number of units, and the tentative timeline. If this went forward, those houses could be occupied as early as the following summer. "Before I continue, Councilwoman Livingston, as I understand you are an investor in this development, you will need to be recused."

Judy rose from her seat and proceeded to the front of the audience, taking the opposite end of the row from Wyatt.

Wyatt slouched in his seat, his arm draped the chair back next to him. Judy assumed a similarly confident posture. The two of them had schemed together for the biggest deal in this town since the gold rush over a century ago. People would do anything for money.

The mayor finished recapping the proposal. He looked up at Wyatt. "Mr Smith, I'm going to turn the meeting over to you. Would you now please conduct a review of your plans as submitted? We're especially interested in those areas where your proposal is dependent upon other parcels in the area."

Wyatt nodded and proceeded to the podium. He plopped the file down on the table next to him. He unrolled the property map and placed it on an easel to the side of the room. With a laser pointer he described the perimeter of the four hundred and twenty acres. I saw from my vantage point a portion of hotel property was clearly part of their plans. Max's identification of those trees was spot on. It was apparent that the Cedarbrook Trails property would be partially taken over by the development as well.

Judy stood and leaned toward the chart. She looked at Wyatt and returned to her seat. "Do I understand you correctly that the project you've proposed will cover part of the Cedarbrook Trails as well as the Cedarbrook Treehouse hotel?" she asked. Her smile was long gone, replaced by a frown. She was furiously writing notes.

Before the Wyatt could respond, the mayor gaveled three times. "Councilwoman Livingston, you are recused. Therefore, you are not allowed comment during this period."

Wyatt continued, "That's correct. It's all there in the approval papers," he replied, gesturing toward the council.

Judy ripped a single sheet of paper from her pile she had taken with her. She turned it around and held it with both hands for Wyatt and the council to see. "You mean this one?" she asked.

The gavel slam startled her. She looked at the mayor and he glared back. Receiving the message, Judy sat back in her seat.

"Please continue, Mr. Smith," the mayor said.

"If that's the project approval letter, then yes," Wyatt replied. He shifted his weight between his feet. "So with that approval, I'd like to proceed with the final piece of financial review. If you'll go to section three, I'll start with the investor data." He grabbed a notebook, placed it on the podium, and flipped through the pages.

Judy held up her hand. "Whoa! Before you do that, we need to look at this approval. The original application didn't say anything about taking the other properties mentioned. Is there another approval letter in this package with those details?"

The mayor crossed his arms and shook his head, losing the battle to keep Judy in check.

Wyatt pointed to the piece of paper in Judy's hand. "It's all in the original right there." He turned and pleaded with the mayor to shut Judy's comments down. But I didn't think there was any way that bulldozer would stop now.

"We may have to take this topic back to a work session. It looks like there's some discrepancy. Judy, your signature is on the approval. What am I missing?" the mayor said.

Judy turned the piece of paper around, looked down, and gasped. "That's my signature. But I would never approve taking the additional property for this project. I value the history and natural beauty here too much to do that."

Wyatt pulled out another piece of paper and waved it. "Since we obviously have the approvals, I'd like to proceed with the financial review." He looked at the mayor and received his assent to continue.

Judy slumped in her seat and shook her head. She was clearly blind-sided by his proposal. I couldn't understand why she wasn't more upbeat. Wouldn't a bigger development benefit her even more from a financial standpoint?

Wyatt continued, "I admit, we've certainly had our challenges with investors. With Everett Landon pulling out at the last minute, we had to scramble. But we finally have a solid set on board. Enough to proceed."

Judy returned to her full-seated position. The dollar signs in her eyes now gleamed. The almighty buck overruled any objection she had to the proposal taking property from other owners.

The mayor continued, "Why don't you walk us through phase one?"

"Of course," Wyatt said. "The initial location of phase one is solely on the property initially purchased. This way, we can provide for those who need time to adjust to the expansion by the time we are in phase two."

Judy wiggled in her seat.

"Can you run the numbers for us on the total and then by phase?" Councilman Ford asked.

Judy preened as Wyatt detailed how she would be profiting. I didn't begrudge her a return on her investment. But when it came at the expense of others, that was too much.

Wyatt flipped through the notebook again. "I'm now looking at section four. The final financials approved by the bank."

The council headed over to that portion of their documents and the mayor nodded to proceed.

"What is this?" Judy stood and shook the paper at Wyatt.

"Order," the mayor said and gaveled.

"You thief!" Judy yelled again, pointing at Wyatt.

The mayor gaveled several times. "Councilwoman Livingston. Please contain yourself or you'll be excused."

"But Mayor! Wyatt Smith has not only forged my signature on the approval, but he's scammed me out of my share of the project. The financials show him and his investors as the sole owners. My contribution and ownership are nowhere to be found. How could you!?" Judy's voice now escalated.

Wyatt returned all of his papers to his folder. "Your honor, Councilwoman Livingston is obviously upset. And I feel she's too close to this project to cast a final vote. I respectfully request she be removed from the remainder of the meeting."

"With Violet out of the way, we were home free. How dare you take advantage of my good nature for your own benefit. Without me, you'd be nowhere. I know you wanted Violet gone because she threatened to out your illegal dealings. I can't prove it, but I'm sure you killed her." Judy plopped in her chair, dropped the papers, and buried her head in her hands.

"Councilwoman Livingston! For the last time, conduct yourself in a professional manner or you will be removed." The mayor's face reddened. No wonder he wanted out. This amount of drama in a small town? He probably ran for the position thinking he might only be involved in the occasional ribbon-cutting ceremony. The mayor dropped the gavel and threw his hands in the air as surrender.

It had now dawned on Judy that she had been Wyatt's pawn in his diabolical scheme. But he was in much deeper than just scamming people out of their money. I had to act quickly to alert Buzz.

I returned to the room and approached the mayhem. "I've already called the police. Wyatt, I know you were the last person to see Violet alive. You were overheard having an argument with her at the same time she was scheduled to pick up her dog from grooming. And the next thing we know, she's dead in the lobby of Pearl's."

He shook his head. "You don't know what you're talking about. That troublemaker was bad for this town and its future. This development is the best thing to happen in the last century."

"Can you explain why you had one of Violet's protest signs in the back seat of your car?" I continued, grilling him like I was a professional interrogator. I shakily moved further toward the front of the room. Was I taking my life in my hands in the presence of an alleged murderer?

He shook his head and hurried down the aisle to the exit, leaving his briefcase behind. "You don't know what you're talking about. I did you all a favor."

The mayor jumped up and sprinted after Wyatt. There might just be a take down in the lobby of city hall. As one of his remaining official acts, the mayor tackled Wyatt. I heard sirens in the distance.

Judy had her head down, sobbing. I felt confident the development as we knew it would never see the light of day. Just like Wyatt after he was convicted.

CHAPTER FIFTEEN

It had been a few weeks since the council meeting. They had done right by Violet. A portion of the Cedarbrook Trails had been dedicated as a dog park. It was quite the sight to see all of those pups running their hearts out in this space. Mom and I strolled the walking path along the perimeter as Max and Trixie romped with some new friends. This was such a great way for them to expend a bunch of pent-up energy. With all of my time attending numerous town council meetings to chauffeur the hotel expansion proposal through the process, Max had been antsy to get out. He would certainly be ready for one of Pearl's classic dog massages when he was done. He deserved that, and more, for helping solve Violet's murder.

Mom kicked a pebble. "I'm so mad I didn't see through Wyatt's slimy exterior before he hurt Joey. I'm usually a pretty good judge of character."

The dirt path was beginning to get a little muddy due to a recent rainstorm. We continued our walk, dodging mud puddles. "Nobody saw through it. That's how it is with those shysters. They're so slick, they even convince themselves that what they're doing is right, or for the greater good."

Trixie bounded over to Mom, who reached down to pet her. I was grateful Mom had her as a companion since I'd moved out of her house and into the hotel. "It's just too bad Violet had to pay with her life before we discovered it."

I called Max over so we could leash them up and head out. "I'm just glad Max was able to find some clues that led me to the answers. If he hadn't seen those trees marked for destruction, Wyatt may have gotten away with it."

Mom clasped Trixie's leash to her harness and we headed to the exit. Our pups' tongues lolled far out of their mouths. The rest of the dogs converged on us to say goodbye. I reached down to pet a couple. This place would definitely be on our frequent visit list.

I got the water and bowls out of the car to give the dogs a quick drink. They slurped them dry.

"Chloe, what's the big surprise you mentioned?" Mom asked.

I loaded the dogs into the back seat. "Actually, I have two."

Mom and I got in and buckled up for the ride home. "Well, don't keep me in suspense. What are they?"

I looked at her before I started the car. "We've been approved for the hotel expansion. We can add those two new units. So start thinking of names. And the lodge has also been approved as part of it."

She squealed. Max and Trixie jumped up and started barking. Everyone approved of the plans. "OK, you guys, settle down." They stopped barking but continued bouncing around the seat. I had no idea how they still had any energy to move at all. I started the car and headed out of the parking lot.

"With all of that space we can host larger events, which means more money for the hotel. This is really going to bring in new business to help us and the town too. I've already got plans to market to Emerald Hills and beyond. It's a pretty big project, but I'm ready."

"Did you just hint at the second surprise?" Mom's voice caught in her throat as she placed a hand on my arm.

I shook my head yes and looked at her. Tears formed in her eyes. The dogs stood and started barking again. I was fully convinced they understood humans. "Yes, Mom. I'm moving back."

"Oh, Chloe." She was speechless, not an easy feat to accomplish with my mom.

I turned into Mom's neighborhood. "It's the right time. Starting a big project at the hotel, it makes sense for me to be there."

"My family is finally becoming whole again. Now, all I need is Harrison. Maybe you can convince him." She removed her hand from my arm and placed it in her lap. "Would you talk to him?"

I hesitated. Never say never, but I couldn't see any path forward to Harrison's return to town. He and his family were firmly established elsewhere. A visit, maybe. But completely moving back? Although, maybe closer in another town could be a compromise. I'd see what I could do.

I pulled into Mom's driveway to deposit her and Trixie before Max and I returned to the hotel. I couldn't wait to collapse with my boy and settle in for a huckleberry vodka and a new puzzle, one that didn't involve someone dying.

"Yes. I will. And I'll have to take a road trip so I can get all of my things and put my house up for sale."

"Chloe, I don't remember when I've been this happy. Thank you."

I gave her a big hug. Max reached into the front seat and put both paws around her for a hug too. I got out and escorted them to the front door. I had no idea what I was getting myself into with a permanent return to this town and overseeing a major construction project. But what is life, if not an adventure? And this would be a whole new world for Max and me.

BUTTERCUPS AND BETRAYAL

A TREEHOUSE HOTEL COZY MYSTERY
(BOOK 3)

SUE HOLLOWELL

CHAPTER ONE

Every light blazed in the normally dark Cedarbrook Historical Museum as Mom and I pulled into the parking lot. I maneuvered my car into a parking space as my mother eyed the bright, busy building from the passenger seat.

"They really pulled out all the stops tonight," she said, but the way she grumbled made it sound more like an insult than a compliment.

"Well, it's a big deal," I said, trying to keep the mood chipper. Mom had been critical of the museum's handling of the town history for a long time. "It's been a long time since we've added a new piece to our small-town collection."

I parked and helped her out of the car, and together, we walked to the front door. The two-story brick building was a historic landmark in the community, and had really been revitalized these last few years, especially recently with the appointment of a new curator. Tonight, the doors were propped open, and people milled about in the lobby, inspecting the displays and the buffet of hors d'oeuvres.

But Mom would not be sidetracked. She steered me through the double doors at the other end of the lobby and into the auditorium. Empty chairs lined the aisles. At the far end, a heavy, velvet curtain hid the new artifact from view. Much to Mom's dismay, it was guarded by Angela.

Angela wore a period costume, displaying a full-length, long-sleeved dress covered by a pinafore apron. Above her pioneer-woman boots I saw the ruffles of bloomers. And to top it off, she wore a prairie bonnet over her bright red hair.

"Hi Chloe, Mabel." She greeted us with hugs. Angela was married to my nephew at one point, and she stayed close to my sister through the years. Now, she was a supervisor here at the museum. It was the perfect position for her. She could recite the town history by heart and had endless stories about each piece owned by the museum.

"You won't let me get a peek, will you?" Mom asked, trying to lean around Angela. She was somewhat of a collector herself, hoarding several items in the hotel office that she refused to donate to the museum in spite of many valiant attempts by the staff through the years.

Angela laughed good-naturedly. "Unfortunately not, but here, these front-row seats are available. Best seats in the house."

We settled into the seats she offered.

"I'm going to go try to find Mr. Higgons so we can get started soon," Angela said. As she walked back up the aisle to hunt for the curator, her skirts swished around her ankles.

The seat beside me was quickly filled by a chubby woman with short, black hair carrying an over-sized, leopard-print purse. The woman leaned around me and greeted my mother.

"Mabel, good to see you here."

My mom gave her a cursory glance. "Donna." Then, to me, she said, "Chloe, this is Donna. She's on the board of the museum."

I shook Donna's hand. When she withdrew, she dug into her purse, extracting a butterscotch candy, which she offered to us. Mom declined, but I accepted her gift with thanks, if only not to be rude.

Donna looked around at the crowd. "Our little museum is really making a name for itself, don't you think? Bart Higgons has been just an invaluable addition to the team."

I glanced over my shoulder. "I think Angela went looking for him. We didn't see him when we came in."

Donna dismissed the comment with a wave of her hand. "He'll be here. It's a big day for him, after all."

But when I saw Angela hurrying down the aisle beside a severe-looking woman in a tailored pantsuit, I had my doubts. The woman climbed the stairs to the stage and took what was supposed to be Bart's place behind the podium. The crowd hushed as she began to speak, the microphone crackling a bit at first.

"Welcome, Cedarbrook. I'm Judy Livingston. Many of you may know me as the mayor of our little town."

As Judy paused while people clapped, Mom leaned around me to Donna. "What were you saying about Bart?"

Donna waved her away again.

The mayor continued, "I'm pleased to welcome you tonight to our growing little gem of a museum, putting us on the map of the national tour of museums. This is due, in no small part, to the stellar curator I hired to develop this place into an award-winning destination. At the moment, we are unable to locate Bart Higgons, so we'll begin the program."

Judy pulled a piece of paper from a folder and began reading. She described the new piece in the museum as the oldest-known functioning water canteen in existence from the pioneers exploring the west. She finished detailing the piece, handed her paper and folder to her assistant, and grabbed the cord to the curtain. She tugged on the heavy drape to slowly reveal the display in a dramatic fashion.

With a couple of tugs, the display was in full view.

And so was Bart Higgons's body on the floor in front of the bench.

Spotlights blazed over the scene. Gasps filled the room. Someone rushed forward to check Bart's pulse before looking up at Judy. "He's dead," he announced.

Beside me, Mom gasped and grabbed my hands, squeezing with her bony fingers. At the base of the stage, Angela clapped her hands over her mouth.

"Maybe we should go," I whispered to my mom.

"Not on your life," she bit back.

Judy rushed in. "The canteen's missing," she yelled. Then, seeming to realize her callous response, she tried to recover. "Poor Bart. And he was doing so well here. Who could do such a thing?"

Angela seemed to shake off her surprise and started taking charge. She gave two sharp claps of her hands to get the crowd's attention, and then started herding all the rubberneckers up the aisle and back to the lobby where they could gossip to their hearts' content until the police arrived. There would probably even be new arrivals once the news spread. The joys of small-town living.

I stood and helped Mom to her feet. Donna had already vacated the seat beside me and gathered with the small crowd around Bart's body.

My mom was handling things in her normal fashion, grumbling as she gathered her purse. "I came out for a nice evening," she said, "and now this." She gazed with disgust at the body on the stage.

For once, I agreed with her.

This was definitely not the night we had planned.

CHAPTER TWO

Mom and I were on our way out, bringing up the tail end of the crowd, when Angela returned, snagging me by my shoulder. "Please don't leave," she whispered. "I can't deal with—" She stopped, her eyes going wide as she looked over my shoulder.

"Unbelievable," came Judy's sharp voice. We all turned to see her still on the stage, her wide, dark eyes narrowed on Angela. "I knew you'd make trouble if we didn't select you for the curator position."

Angela took a step back as if from the force of the accusation. "I did not!" she objected.

Judy, trailed by Donna, marched up the aisle. Trapped, I nudged Mom into one of the rows to get out of the way. From here, I could see sweat beading on Angela's brow, but I felt it was probably more thanks to the layers of heavy clothing she wore than to any guilty conscience.

Angela wasn't family anymore, but I knew her, and I knew she wasn't capable of murder.

At least, I thought she wasn't. She was singularly devoted to her daughter.

"Now, hold on just a minute," I interjected. "I think we need to call the Emerald Hills police and get them down here to do the investigating before we start pointing fingers."

But my objections fell on deaf ears. The mayor whirled on Donna, who held her leather bag in front of her like a shield. "And you. I had a feeling Bart was trouble, but you insisted on hiring him."

"I did no such thing," Donna objected. As she talked, the hard candy she sucked on clacked against her teeth. "You knew full well his background and the rumors about his shady dealings. Your decisions are always tainted by the almighty buck. All you could talk about was how Bart's museum expansion plans would bring more money in."

"Shady dealings?" my mom whispered to me.

I shrugged as Donna and Judy continued to trade jabs.

"When the museum board meets next week, I'll be petitioning to have you removed." Judy paced in front of the stage, Bart's body behind her, largely unacknowledged. "The only reason you're there is because you wormed your way in by saying you're a collector." Judy made air quotes around the word collector.

Donna shook her head and smirked. "You wouldn't know a historical collectible if it hit you over the head. At least I knew what Bart was talking about when he proposed acquiring new pieces."

The crowd was now long gone. The yelling echoed off the tall, exposed beam ceilings. With Judy and Donna going at each other, this seemed like the perfect time to make our escape. Slipping out of the row, I grabbed Angela's hand.

"Chloe, you've got to help me. I had nothing to do with this," Angela said. "If I lose this job, I'll never get my daughter back."

I placed my hand on Angela's back and softly said, "I'll do what I can." I looked over at the curtain. Someone had lowered it, disguising the evening's tragedy, but I knew the impact of the murder was just beginning.

As I ushered Mom and Angela from the room, Mom took up her grumbling again. "This is why I won't let the museum have any of my things. They tell me they care about the history, and then something like this happens."

I said goodbye to Angela, promising to help where I could, and opened the door for Mom to get into the car. By the time I sat down and started the car, I was exhausted. This was the type of night where I couldn't wait to hang out with my cuddly cocker spaniel and forget the craziness of the world for at least a few hours.

CHAPTER THREE

That night, after dropping Mom off, I made my way to the Buttercup Bungalow treehouse unit that had become our home over the last few months. It was technically part of the hotel my mom owned and had been the first room we'd decorated together. It looked like the home decor store had exploded in here, but I loved how bright and warm it was. It likely wasn't a permanent arrangement, but right now, the peace and tranquility of the forest was exactly what I needed.

Max and I snuggled up on the small loveseat in the front room, my huckleberry vodka cocktail and Max's ginger treats on the table, along with a new puzzle ready for solving.

I placed my feet on the ottoman, opened the puzzle book, and got out my pencil. Our puzzle preference was for numbers, not words. Not that I didn't like word search or a simple crossword, but my brain somehow gravitated toward the logic. Our new adventure tonight was a KenKen puzzle. It was similar to our usual sudoku but with the extra factor of computation. We'd start on an easy one until we learned the techniques to master the more complex.

The way this worked with Max was that I would read the clues out loud and he would tap on the page with his answer. I would confirm the number and he would shake his head yes or no. It was going to be fun to see how he did adding math to the picture.

I stroked his silky brown fur as I read the first clue. I always waited for him to answer first. After a long pause, he raised his paw, placed it on the book and looked at me, appearing unconfident in his answer. I hoped he didn't think I was trying to trick him.

I laughed. "You got it, boy," I said.

He smiled that mile-wide Muppet grin, pleased with his accomplishment.

I took a turn at the second clue. He watched me write the number in the book. When he saw what it was, he nodded his head. So much for the beginner level. As always, Max was a quick study.

I petted his head. "This isn't our only puzzle to solve. Somehow, Bart at the museum ended up dead on opening night of the reveal of the new collection. And the canteen is missing."

He stood and wagged his tail, always ready to tackle another mystery.

"Ah, not now. But I definitely need your help," I said.

He returned to his puzzle-solving position.

I read the next clue to him, he pointed to the number, and looked at me again. *Spot on, Max. We might have to go to the next level of difficulty right now.*

Max and I continued tag teaming the puzzle. We finished the first one and moved on to a second. He scooted closer to me, almost halfway into my lap. I took that as a sign that he liked the KenKen.

But I was distracted, the mystery of the murder weighing heavy on my mind, especially with Angela as a potential suspect.

"I know Bart was a divisive figure in this community, even though he'd only been in town less than a year," I said. "With that scene at the museum the night of the murder, I couldn't tell if Judy or Donna liked Bart or not. I think they liked what he did for the museum, but maybe not how he went about it." I looked down at Max, certain by now he understood my words. We had worked enough puzzles, including solving murders, that I knew we were in sync.

I leaned down and gave him a hug with my left arm. He was such a calming influence when needed.

"We're going to have to learn a little more about Bart. What do you say we start on that tomorrow?"

Max leapt up like he'd seen a bunny he wanted to chase. He barked once and wagged that stubby little tail so hard I thought it would fly off his body.

Just then, my phone vibrated. I picked it up off the table and studied the caller ID before answering. It was my sister, Angela's ex-mother-in-law. I was sure she'd heard everything by now.

I put the puzzle book and pencil on the table and answered the phone. "Hi, Joey. How are you holding up?"

"I'm just so worried about Angela," she said, starting right in. "She's almost inconsolable." Joey's normally freewheeling personality was now all business.

"I'm sorry, Joey. That has to be horrible for her. And for you," I added.

Angela had been married to my sister Joey's son, Brady, but it had been a tumultuous relationship, mostly because Brady always seemed to find trouble. They'd had a daughter together, Samantha, but Angela didn't currently have custody until she could move into a bigger place.

"She was on track to have Sam back in her home again. If she'd gotten the curator position, that would have given her enough money to get her own place," Joey said. "I just don't know what to do. Do you think you can help?"

Max put his chin on my thigh and gazed up at me, his large, brown eyes somber. Absently, I stroked his head. "I don't know a lot about Bart, but Max and I will ask around and see what we can do."

Joey's voice cracked. "I know it looks bad for her, but I'm sure Angela had nothing to do with Bart's death. She's a good mom to Sam and would never do anything to jeopardize getting her back."

"This won't be easy. I'll keep you posted," I said.

We exchanged our goodbyes and hung up. I returned the phone to the table and looked at Max. He ever so quietly whimpered, his jowls drooping.

"I agree. It's sad for so many reasons."

Max's eyes diverted to the table on my right and the plate of ginger treats. His gaze returned to mine, requesting permission to dig in. We needed to fuel up if we were moving full-on into murder-solving mode. I nodded my head. The predictability of his penchant toward ginger warmed my heart.

He stood and carefully tiptoed across my lap to retrieve a cookie. He snagged one, returned to his seat, and quietly munched. We both enjoyed our goodies and pondered our mission to find Bart's killer, locate the missing museum collectible, and clear Angela's name.

I placed the book of KenKen puzzles on the table, saving them for another day.

CHAPTER FOUR

The air had started to turn crisp in the mornings, hinting at fall. Mom and I were meeting Paul this morning at the hotel to do a walk-through of the initial construction plans for our expansion. The two new units and the lodge were the biggest changes that had happened to this place since it was initially built. Mom and I had been redecorating the existing units like crazy so we would be ready for the two new ones. Mom was pleased as punch that she got to name them. I was a bit hesitant, given how she could go a little sideways with things at times. But Crocus Castle and Dogwood Den fit perfectly with the theme of the existing treehouses. And Lily Lodge gave us so much potential for decorating ideas that we already had some of the curtains purchased.

I heard the crunch of gravel from the driveway and assumed that would be Paul, the construction manager for our project. Since my return to Cedarbrook, I had become reacquainted with many of the residents I knew from my youth and met quite a few new ones. Paul had come recommended from Pearl, where he had put in some upgrades at her Pearl's Pooch Pampering business.

I stood and peered through the small window. "Mom, I think Paul's here."

She was seated in a corner, flipping through a decorating magazine. She had acquired quite a stack of those in preparation for our new project. "OK, dear." She continued perusing with her head down.

"I think he wants us to walk around with him to tour the site where they'll be building." I tried to budge her from her focus. No luck.

"You can do that. You don't need me," she said.

I shrugged and opened the door to greet Paul. I didn't expect to see what I found on the other side. Paul was about six feet tall, cropped white hair, and a salt-and-pepper scruffy beard. He wore a plaid flannel shirt over heavy duty construction pants and work boots.

Mom bolted out of her chair like it had caught fire. She was at my side in about one-second flat, reaching out to shake his hand before he was even in the door. And Max was right behind her. You would think she had never seen a handsome man before.

"I'm Mabel, the owner of this hotel. Nice to meet you," she said.

He laughed, easing the awkward tension. "Hello, Mabel, nice to meet you as well."

I stepped away from the door to let him in. "Mom, why don't you let Paul in for a minute before we do our tour?" I said.

She let go of his hand and stepped to the side to make room for his entry. Taking her place in the doorway, Max stepped in to greet Paul. He bent over and gave Max a good scratch behind his ears. Max turned and bounded over to me, with obvious approval of Paul.

"That's quite the welcoming committee," Paul said, chuckling. "I think I'm going to really enjoy this project, for lots of reasons." Paul stepped inside, and I closed the door.

Mom eyeballed me behind Paul's back. I ignored her look. No way was I ready for a boyfriend. It didn't matter how handsome he was. I had a job to do. And when Max and I weren't busy at the hotel, we had a murder to solve.

"I've brought the plans with me, but I thought we could look at the site first to talk about how this is going to happen," Paul said. He set the large roll of architecture drawings on the guest registration desk.

Mom and Max returned to front and center, both of them with matching goofy grins on their faces. I avoided eye contact or I would've never been able to get through this.

"OK," I said. "Mom, let's get our coats and head out. We can talk about the decorations later."

She was as giddy as a schoolgirl. I knew how her mind worked. She already had Paul and me married. She practically skipped to get her jacket and followed us outside. Max galloped alongside us. I wasn't sure if it was because he got to go outside or he was happy to have a new friend, or both.

We traversed the path around the center firepit and gathering place, just beyond the Morning Glory Manor. I rubbed my arms to warm up.

Paul gestured to the open area just beyond the circle of units we currently had in operation. "This is where we're going to build Dogwood Den. We've got these two gorgeous pine trees situated in a way that we can incorporate both of them into the treehouse. One of them is in a position to be the center. And the second one is going to be the corner of the outside deck."

Mom, Max, and I craned our necks up to look in the direction Paul pointed toward the tops of the trees. This would be one of the tallest units and have one of the best views. Max and I might have to move here from the Buttercup Bungalow.

Paul continued the path about a hundred yards to the east where Crocus Castle would be.

I reached over to hold Mom's elbow. "Be careful with your step, Mom. It's starting to get a little slippery." For some reason, she wore shoes today that were good for traipsing through the woods. It was usually about what looked good rather than functionality.

Paul had stopped and waited for us. "This is Crocus Castle's new home." He beamed. "I can't wait to get started on these. It's going to be a fun project. Do you have any questions right now?"

I looked at Mom. That grin had returned to her face. I gave a small shake of my head, hoping Paul didn't notice. She would never stop being a matchmaker. "I don't think so. Let's head back inside and warm up with some coffee as we look over the plans."

We turned and retraced our steps back to the office. As we approached the door, I saw Max buried in a bush up to his rear, that stubby little tail practically spinning like a propeller. "C'mon, Max," I said and patted my leg. He didn't budge. If anything, his tail wagged faster. "Max!" Whatever had his attention must have been fascinating. He pulled his head out and looked at me. So many leaves were attached to his head it looked like he was wearing a crown. "Let's go inside." He relented, not wanting to leave his prey. The squirrels at the hotel had been more prevalent lately, appearing to be getting ready for winter. I thought they were taunting Max, but he had a ball chasing them as they escaped up the trees.

We got inside and I started a pot of coffee. Max fawned all over Paul, bonding with his new friend. Paul started picking the leaves from Max's fur. "That fur is like Velcro for sticks and leaves," he said.

I got three cups out and set them next to the coffee pot. "It's a constant battle," I said. "But well worth it for my buddy."

"So Paul, tell us about yourself." Mom put her jacket on the hook by the door.

Oh boy, here we go. I stepped over to the building plans and began unrolling the paper. "Mom, let's look over the plans while we wait for our coffee."

She shook her head. "Chloe, you don't have to be all business, all the time."

Paul came to the desk to wrangle the paper rolls and lay them out so we could see them. He looked up at me with those warm brown eyes. My face began to heat up. I grabbed the stapler to hold down one corner of the papers.

Paul pulled the reservation book over to weigh down the opposite side of the plans. "I can't tell you how much I appreciate your business too. This has been my dream for some time," he said.

"I'm glad it worked out for us too," Mom said and joined us at the desk. She looked at me and smiled, not disguising her intent one bit. I felt like my whole body would catch fire from the heat igniting inside of me. She and I were going to have a direct conversation after Paul left. No fixing me up.

"If I hadn't gotten your project, I'd likely have gone out of business. Or at least had to put a hold on things while I returned to my previous job as a delivery driver. Not that I didn't like it, but getting up at four o'clock every day wore me out," he said.

"I saw what you did at Pearl's. You do good work." My flushed cheeks remained. I really hoped he didn't notice. I wiped my clammy hands on my pants.

"It's just that the big contract I had with the museum for their new wing got canceled," Paul said. "I'm still not sure why. But it would have sustained me for almost a year. I don't want to speak ill of the dead, especially since there's suspicious circumstances, but I feel like Bart had it out for me."

Something didn't sound right about that. Paul seemed like an awfully nice person. And if he was a decent businessman, why would Bart do that?

Max sauntered over to join us, placed his front paws on the desk, and looked over the plans. He was ready for the meeting to begin.

"Well, it's lucky for us that happened. Otherwise we wouldn't be working with you for our project. Right, Chloe?" Mom asked.

Deep down Mom was a romantic at heart. With all of her husbands I felt like she was just looking for love. And now she was on a mission to find that for me. Mercy.

CHAPTER FIVE

O ur little town library was anything but quiet this evening. The gathering place for tonight's bingo tournament teemed with people setting up the room. This event was one of the biggest moneymakers for the high school scholarships. Most of the proceeds went to seniors pursuing some type of education after high school. The tables were arranged in rows facing the front of the room, where the bingo caller would stand. A raised platform had been brought in. Behind the platform was a large board to display numbers as they were called. This was serious business.

Mom and I surveyed the room as we arrived. "Where would you like to sit?" I asked her.

She looked all around, assessing the choices for the best spot. "How about the second row, toward the middle aisle?"

"Sounds good. That way it will be easy for you to go collect your winnings."

She had her game face on. I knew bingo was a game of chance, but Mom still wanted to win, if only for bragging rights. We wove our way past all of the chairs to her prime location. "Let's put our stuff down to save our seats and go purchase our cards," she said.

Max jumped up into a chair and Mom and I put our purses down, one on each side of him. My boy loved number puzzles, and I just knew he would really enjoy playing bingo. We left him and went to the table on the side to load up on cards.

"Hi Victor," Mom said. "We'll take the maximum number of cards each."

Victor counted off twenty cards from the giant stacks in front of him. "Here you go," he said. "Good luck."

"We'll need twenty more," I said. "Max is playing tonight too." I gestured back toward our table location where Max was exhibiting his best manners.

Victor peered around me and frowned. "I don't understand," he said, and looked back and forth between Mom and me.

Explaining Max's number smarts to people always sent them off kilter. "Yes, he's playing tonight too," I said.

Victor tipped his head. "Really?"

I nodded.

Victor counted off twenty more cards and handed them to me, his eyebrows raised.

"I'm sorry about Bart," Mom said.

Victor's shoulders slumped. He opened his mouth and closed it again. His chin wavered. "Thank you," he whispered.

We grabbed three different-colored bingo daubers, one for each of us, and returned to our seats. I placed a pile of cards in front of Max and a pile in front of me.

Mom leaned over to me, past Max, and said, "I feel bad for Victor. He seemed to really care for Bart. Continuing on with the bingo tournament must be hard since it was something they always did together."

Bart and Victor had been dating for quite a few months. Mom had said they met soon after Bart arrived in town. Victor seemed a good match for Bart and seemed to get him, with Bart's sophisticated taste for the finer things.

"It is sad. Hopefully tonight will pick up his spirits a bit. This looks like a lot of fun," I said. "Do you want to grab some snacks before it begins?"

Max looked at me, inquiring about ginger treats. I rubbed his head. "Maybe later, boy."

"I'll just have water and maybe some popcorn," Mom said and sat down.

I headed to the snack table to get our goodies. The room filled quickly with the remaining participants. We were just about to the starting time. I returned to Mom and Max with our supplies and hunkered down for a night of bingo.

"Hi Aunt Chloe and Max and Grannie Mabel," Angela said. She was scooting behind our chairs to reach the end of the table and the last seat to Mom's right side.

"Hi dear. And don't call me Grannie. That makes me sounds old. Please call me Grandma Mabel if you have to use a title," Mom said. She had lined up four cards, ready for game one to begin.

Angela looked over her head at me and smirked. I returned the expression.

"Well hello, Mabel, and everyone." Donna made her way to the seat right in front of us.

Mom raised her head and continued arranging her cards. "Hello," she said.

Donna dropped her purse on the floor and started placing her cards in front of her, ready for battle. This was supposed to be for fun and to support the kids.

"Ladies and gentlemen, I want to welcome you to our annual bingo tournament for scholarships," Judy said. If anyone was born to be in front of a crowd, it was her. Even if she had no audience, I think she'd pontificate as if she did. "This is the best turnout we've ever had. I'm expecting this to be the largest amount of scholarships we're awarding to our dear children."

Max coughed, not something I had seen him do very often.

Judy stopped and glared at the source of the noise.

I snickered.

She turned her gaze back to the crowd. "Continuing on. Thank you for coming and good luck. I'm going to turn it over to Victor to let the games begin," Judy dramatically ended. She returned the microphone to the stand on the table for Victor's use in calling the numbers.

He stepped up, turning the bingo cage and said, "Get ready everyone."

Mom grabbed the dauber like she was arming for battle, elbow out, poised.

"First number. B nine," Victor said slowly, articulating every syllable. "B nine," he repeated and placed the ball in the holder on the wall behind him.

Max tapped me on the arm. I looked over at his card and saw he had the number. I picked up his dauber and marked it. He smiled at me.

"Next number. I twenty-three," Victor spoke loudly into the microphone. "I twenty-three."

"C'mon," I heard Mom mumble, her head bowed over her cards, arm in the air with the dauber ready.

Victor continued announcing three more numbers when the first winner of the night shouted, "Bingo!"

Angela jumped up from her chair and speed walked to the front of the room. She handed Victor her card, he nodded, and reviewed the numbers. "We have our first winner, ladies and gentlemen."

Angela made eye contact with him again and smiled.

"Well, that couldn't have been any faster," Donna loudly said. "Five numbers?"

"That's all it takes," Angela said as she swiped by Donna on the return to her seat.

"OK, everyone. Let's get ready for round two," Victor said. We continued that way through round ten and to the intermission.

Max tapped me on the elbow several times throughout the games. But for only about half of those did he have a number on his card. Maybe it would take a few tournaments before he started to get the hang of it.

Donna turned around in her seat to chat Mom up during our break. "Mabel, I'm telling you, you would have loved that last cruise I went on. You should seriously think about going with me sometime."

Mom looked at me like Donna had just told her she had three heads. "I think Donna's right. You should do that, Mom. You work hard and you deserve it. With me here taking care of the hotel, you should take some time for yourself."

"Well, you're no help, Chloe. I'm not rich like you, Donna. I can't afford things like that big, fancy Gucci purse you have or going on cruises every other week," Mom replied.

Donna's hand dropped to her purse on the floor next to her. "I bought that with my gambling winnings. Just think about it, OK?" Donna asked.

Mom shrugged.

"We're going to get started again," Victor announced. "Please grab your seats,"

I positioned mine and Max's remaining cards. Even if we didn't win, it had been fun.

Victor called three more games, and Max continued to tap my arm. He was still about fifty-fifty having the correct number. I wasn't sure why he hadn't grasped the pattern. Maybe there were too many distractions. With only a few games left, Max tapped my arm again.

He turned in his seat and looked at me, straight on. He was trying to communicate something. I wish I understood his mannerisms as much as he understood mine.

I petted him. "What is it, boy?" I whispered.

He tapped his card. I pointed to one of the numbers. He nodded his head yes. I still didn't get it. He tapped me again and I pointed to another number. He nodded again. Now I was starting to catch on. Max had noticed a pattern where some numbers had never been called. Was he trying to tell me that he thought Victor was cheating? Why would Victor do that? Taking money from the scholarships? Max had to be mistaken. But how could I know for sure?

We were on the home stretch with the next-to-last game coming up. Max's accusation distracted me from daubing our cards. He continued to tap me, now more called numbers appearing on his card. With only one more number, G sixty, Max would have a bingo.

As if willing it, Victor called, "G sixty." He paused. "G sixty."

Max looked at me and began barking. My boy that had been silent as a mouse the entire time was now making a spectacle of himself. And rightly so. He had just won a bingo game. I daubed the last number, he grabbed the card, and trotted up to Victor, dropping it at his feet.

Victor picked it up by the corner and verified it was a winner. Everyone clapped, and Max turned and faced the audience, taking it all in. He leapt from the platform and sprinted back to his seat, ready for our last game.

We finished that last round without another win. But Max would ride that high from his victory for quite a while.

CHAPTER SIX

Max and I looked forward to a nice, relaxing stroll in the dog park. At least it would be relaxing for me. Every time Max came, he romped until his tongue almost touched the ground. I was glad to be able to bring him to a place to play with other dogs. He hung around me so much, he sometimes seemed more human than canine. Ever since the park had been built, it was a busy place. The setup provided a walking path around the fenced perimeter and lots of play space in the middle.

I leashed up Max as we exited the car until we got inside the park. We entered through the gate, I unleashed him, and he took off like a rocket, greeting his long-lost friends. The longer I was in town, the more I got reacquainted with people I hadn't seen in years, and the more new friends I made. I was sure I would see someone I knew at the park. I began my stroll and took in the gorgeous territorial views across the valley. The fresh air cleansed my lungs and cleared my head. I took a deep breath and thought about the events of the last few days. I needed some time to sort out what was going on with Bart's death. Still not much news from the Emerald Hills PD, either.

"Chloe, wait up, and I'll walk with you."

I turned around and saw Kathleen Timmons. She had just released her beagle into the play area. If I didn't have my cocker spaniel, I would definitely get a beagle. I waited for her to catch up. I hadn't known Kathleen before I moved back to Cedarbrook. She was Caroline's younger sister and always wanted to hang around with us in high school.

"It's nice to see you again," I said.

We began our walk around the path. "Likewise," she said.

We approached the corner, and I looked for Max in the pack of dogs to be sure everyone was behaving. There were a few tussles now and then, but mostly the dogs just chased each other. Many of the other owners brought toys and things to throw for their dogs, which gave everyone a workout.

"That was a lot of fun last night at bingo," I said. "It's heartwarming that this town does so much for their kids."

We kept to a leisurely stroll. "It really is. I was especially glad to see Angela win a few times. She needs the money, and I know it boosted her spirits after the disaster the other night at the museum," Kathleen said.

I looked at Kathleen. "You guys are friends, right?" I asked.

She smiled. "Yes, our daughters are the same age. We've almost been joined at the hip most of their lives," she said. "I just hope now that Bart's gone, the museum board does the right thing and hires her for the curator position. They should have done that in the first place. Bart didn't deserve that position." Kathleen no longer had a smile on her face. Her pace picked up, and I had to speed up to stay with her.

We rounded the farthest corner from the entry gate. I was glad I was on the inside of the track since it was a little shorter. Any faster and we would be at a jog. "You didn't like Bart?" I asked.

She looked at me, pressing her lips together. Practicing my detective skills, I let the uncomfortable silence stand.

She looked away, her voice deepening. "You could say that."

I waited. We walked the entire length of the park. She was apparently not going to offer anything else without prompting. "He seemed to be doing really well for the museum. I understand it was expanding and he'd been able to acquire some rare pieces for it."

Kathleen stopped, her fists balled. She tilted her head down. "Yeah, things are never what they seem," she said through gritted teeth. She turned and continued the fast pace. I was getting my workout in exchange for this conversation. But if it could provide me some insight into Bart, so be it.

"What do you mean?" I asked, hoping my open-ended questions would keep her talking.

She sighed. I thought this might be the end of this line of questioning. "There's that thing with Angela not getting the museum curator position. But I can't really fault him for that. Although, his shady dealings probably gave him a leg up on being selected. He and my brother were dating. I just didn't like how Victor behaved when it came to Bart. Their relationship seemed to change him, and not in a good way," she said. Her pace slowed a bit.

"I'm sorry." Thankfully, I was able to catch my breath enough to continue the conversation. "It's always tough when a family member makes choices you don't agree with, or that you don't think are in their best interest."

I searched the sea of dogs to make sure Max was still behaving himself. Alone with me, he was angelic. With other dogs? Sometimes that herd mentality got the better of him. I saw him chasing a poodle that looked exactly like a neighbor dog back home. Max and Bruce had become fast friends before we moved to Cedarbrook. Maybe someday we would pay a visit to reacquaint the two.

"Victor really fell hard and fast for Bart. I think he was blinded to Bart's ways. Victor was buying expensive things for Bart with money he didn't have. I don't know how he afforded it. I don't think the extra money he was getting from Angela renting a room was nearly enough to cover those pricey items..." she trailed off.

"I'm sorry, Kathleen. That must have been hard for you to be in the middle like that," I said.

"No matter how many times I tried to talk to him, Victor contradicted every one of my arguments," she said. "There was no cracking that thick skull."

Kathleen's beagle sprinted over to her and sat down, panting. We stopped. Kathleen crouched to pet her dog. I looked over at Max and he showed no signs of slowing down. Ultimately I would have to intervene.

"Eventually, I just had to bite my tongue. Even when I had evidence of Bart's cheating, Victor would have none of it," Kathleen said. She looked at me, sadness in her eyes.

"Sometimes people have to learn the hard way themselves. We just don't want to admit it, even when the truth is staring us in the face," I said.

She stood. "So true. And I wasn't the only one that saw it. It was a public place. I was at Caroline's where Bart was having coffee with Stan. They didn't seem to be trying to hide or anything," she said. "Of course, Bart denied it. Said they were talking business. Which I thought was a good cover story."

We had been at the park about an hour, enough time for Max to exhaust himself.

"I'm sad Bart's dead and that Victor is upset," she said. "But I'm not sad they aren't together anymore. That might make me a horrible person, but those are my feelings."

I called Max over and hooked the leash onto his harness. He obediently sat, ready to go. "I just hope we find out soon what happened so we can all have some peace," I said.

"Me too, Chloe," she replied.

"I'm glad we got to chat. I'll see you soon." I waved goodbye. Max and I made a beeline to the car, both a little wiped out. In his short amount of time in town, Bart had sure developed a complicated life.

CHAPTER SEVEN

The hotel office had started to look like a construction site. Plans were posted on the walls, supplies had been stored in the open spaces. We barely had a walkway to maneuver. I contemplated leaving the pups at Mom's while all of this was underway, but it was a lot of fun having them around.

Paul stopped in again for another update. The treehouses were taking shape, and the frame for the lodge was almost complete. The office door opened and a rush of cool air blew through. Trixie and Max sprinted to greet our guest. They both excitedly yipped and, completely forgoing any manners, jumped all over Paul.

He stopped with the door open, unable to proceed past the welcoming committee.

"Max. Trixie," I said. They completely ignored me and continued their routine. I strode toward the door and clapped my hands three times. Max turned and looked at me, knowing full well my message. Trixie, in her own world, as usual, jumped on Paul for his attention. "Trixie," I said, sternly. I grabbed her harness to disrupt her and let Paul all the way into the office.

He shook his head, a good sport about being mauled. "It could be worse. They might not like me and then we'd have a different scenario on our hands," he said. He closed the door and made his way over to the wall with the plans displayed. I let Trixie go. She and Max sprinted behind Paul. He now had a full entourage.

I followed them to the other side of the room. "Thanks for being so easygoing about it. They can be pretty well-behaved, until they're not. And then they completely lose all composure."

Mom had sauntered up beside me, ready for a status report on the building. "Hi Paul," she said sweetly, looking back and forth between Paul and me. She would not quit.

Paul removed his hat, a gentlemanly gesture. "Hello, Mabel," he said with a giant smile, not missing her intent one bit. Was he on board with this date thing?

This was all starting to be too much. I needed to stick to business, for now.

"I'm excited to share an update with you. Things are going very well," Paul continued.

Mom looked at him, almost glassy-eyed. I was sure there were visions of son-in-law dancing in her head. She looked at me. I completely avoided her eye contact.

Paul pointed to the plan for the Crocus Castle. "This is my favorite. With the A-frame structure, and the wall of windows facing west, the lucky guests in this unit will be able to watch sunsets while sipping a cocktail on the deck," he said.

Mom clasped her hands and held them up to her chin. "Oooo, that sounds so romantic."

I turned my body ever so slightly away from her to try and cut off that line of thinking. "How much longer before we can take a tour?" I asked.

Trixie barked sharply like someone had stepped on her foot. She sprinted toward the door and paced back and forth. I looked at Mom. "Can you hold her until we're done here?" At that moment, Max took off after Trixie, giving her reaction legitimacy.

Mom went to the window, stood on her tiptoes, and peeked out. "I think someone's here," she said. "But I don't see a car." She pulled the door open. Standing right on the other side was Donna with her arm raised as if she was going to knock. Who knocks at a place of business?

Donna lowered her arm and stepped into the office. "Hello, everyone," she said.

Mom closed the door and followed her. "Hi, Donna. What are you doing here?" Mom was nothing, if not to the point.

Donna approached Paul and said, "Hello, there. I'm Donna Sherman. And who are you?"

Paul reached out to shake her hand and said, "I'm Paul York. Nice to meet you."

Mom stepped into their sphere. "Donna, we're in the middle of something."

Donna continued gazing at Paul but acknowledged Mom. "Mabel, I came back to see if you had changed your mind about letting me buy some of your collectible pieces. With Bart no longer at the museum, I would be concerned about you letting that place have any of them."

Mom walked to the coffeemaker and over her shoulder said, "No, thanks. I don't trust anyone else with them." She got a tea bag, put it in a cup, and began filling it with hot water. She took a seat and held the cup, warming her hands.

"We'll let you know if we change our minds. Right now, Paul's plan is to create a beautiful display case in our new lodge to house the pieces," I said. I pointed to Donna's shoes where mud had crept up the sides. "I'm sorry it's so muddy here. I hope it didn't ruin your shoes."

Donna waved a dismissive hand and went to sit with Mom near the coffee pot. "Mabel, have you given any more thought to our conversation the other night at bingo?" Donna asked. "I just returned from a cruise to Alaska. It was spectacular. The views, the glaciers, the wild animals. And there's endless food and entertainment on the ship. You just have to come with me," she said.

Mom's eyes pleaded with me for an intervention. I actually agreed with Donna. Mom could use a break, and she might like a cruise.

"I would be too cold," Mom said to Donna.

Donna looked at me, enlisting my support. "There's other ones where it would be warm and tropical. Say you'll think about it, OK?" Donna asked.

Mom, seeing there was likely no other alternative to getting Donna out of here, agreed to consider it.

Donna jumped up, her large purse swinging to bonk Max on his snout. He barked, looked at me, and shook his head. Oblivious, Donna headed to the door. "Bye, all," she said and left.

Mom got up and joined Paul and me at the plans. "Ugh, that woman is so pushy. I don't know if I could be sequestered with her on a boat for that long."

Max was sniffing Donna's muddy footprints, bringing that to Mom's attention. "And look at the mess she made. I don't think she even wiped her feet," she said.

Um, thanks, Max. "Don't worry. I'll get that later," I said. I turned my attention to Paul. "When do you think we can tour the new units?"

He grinned from ear-to-ear. Yes, the entertainment here was frequent and free. "It shouldn't be too long now," he said.

Max entered the picture and stood right next to Paul.

Paul scratched Max's ears. Max closed his eyes and smiled. "He seems to like me. I hope that's a good sign," he said and looked at Mom. They connected with a conspiratorial look. "Well, I better head outside to check on the crew," he said.

Mom, the pups, and I escorted Paul to the door. As soon as it closed, Mom said, "Chloe, he would be perfect for you."

I hoped if I ignored her, she'd cease her matchmaking, but I was fooling myself. She couldn't help it. And Max had joined forces with her. I'd have to come up with some new avoidance strategies. Not that I wouldn't want to have a love in my life at some point. But just not right now. With Bart's murderer running loose in town, the hotel expansion, not to mention just the day-to-day running of the place, who had time for anything else?

CHAPTER EIGHT

"**M**om, can you try to have an open mind about this?" I asked. Getting her to the travel agent's office was a herculean feat itself, let alone actually choosing a trip to go on. We pulled into the parking lot, I turned off the car and looked at her, waiting for a response. I was hopeful but not optimistic. I really wanted this for her sake. Max whimpered in the back seat. "See, Max thinks you should go too." I reached around and petted him.

Mom opened her door and got out. "Let's just see if Kathleen has anything I like and go from there," she said and closed her door.

Max and I looked at each other and shrugged. Yep, we never knew what to expect from Mabel.

We all headed into Kathleen's office to start the process. Two desks faced the entry doors. Travel posters of faraway places plastered the walls. Every type of location you could imagine was displayed in living color. Along the wall under the windows were several display cases of pamphlets. The visual barrage overwhelmed me. I didn't know how Mom would choose.

Kathleen got up from her desk and came to the other side to greet us. "Hello, everyone. I'm so glad you're here," she said. She gestured to two chairs facing her desk. She returned to her chair, placed her elbows on the desk, hands clasped, and leaned toward us. "So what can I help you with?" she asked.

I looked at Mom. Silence. She wasn't making this easy. Any other person would be jumping at the chance to escape. I looked back at Kathleen. "Mom is interested in exploring cruises," I said.

Kathleen looked at Mom. "OK, great," she replied. "Let's talk a little more about what you might like so I can narrow it down. Then I have some brochures you can look at," she said.

Mom held her purse on her lap like a shield. We waited. Finally, she blurted, "It can't be cold."

Kathleen's excellent customer service came through. "That's a great start," she said. "I have several tropical locations." She got up and gathered a stack of brochures from the racks near the window. She returned to her desk and fanned them out.

I scooted to the edge of my chair to get a better look. If Mom didn't end up going, maybe I would someday. "Do they have cruises where you can bring your dog?" I asked. Max leapt up and placed his snout on the edge of the desk.

Kathleen laughed. "Of course. They have cruises for just about everything and everyone."

I pulled one of the brochures to the edge of the desk in front of Mom. "OK. I'll come back another day to talk more about those. Mom, do you see anything you like?" I asked.

She leaned forward, glancing at the Caribbean pictures. "Hmm. That one does look nice," she said.

Oh, boy. Were we going to play twenty questions for which cruise to pick? "Kathleen, what has Donna done that she's liked?" I asked.

Mom looked at me, her lips pursed. "I probably won't like any of those."

Kathleen looked at Mom. "She's done almost everything. Cruises, bus trips, overseas travel. Her penchant is gambling and museums. So anywhere that takes her to a game of chance or a tour of collectibles, she's in." Kathleen pulled out a pen. "Why don't I show you these brochures one by one, and you can say yes or no. I'll make a list of the ones you like and get you more details on those so you can make a decision. How does that sound?"

No response from Mom. She really was making this difficult. Perhaps we would have to try again another day. "That's an unusual pen," I said, pointing to what Kathleen held in her hand.

She looked at it. "Victor got this for me. They had a limited number made at the museum the last time they had an unveiling with Bart." She paused and looked up. She swallowed and pulled out a pad of paper, then took a deep breath.

"I'm sorry," I said. I hadn't meant to open a wound.

"It's just so fresh," she said quietly. "Well, let's get started on a happier topic." She scooped all of the brochures into a pile and one by one placed them in front of Mom. Mom voted either yes or no, and Kathleen made two more piles. She obviously had experience guiding decisions with people too overwhelmed with all of the choices. I was impressed because Mom was not an easy customer. By the end of the pile Mom had selected four cruises as possibilities. Kathleen began to make a list and write some additional details. She retrieved a folder from her desk drawer and placed the brochures inside.

"Mom, some of those look really nice. I think you're going to enjoy the warmth and being pampered," I said. I hoped my encouragement would help convince her to do this.

"I don't need people to wait on me. I've worked hard all my life and never expected anything from others," she said. That woman was a tough nut to crack. If she wasn't ready, maybe I could convince her to go on a cruise with me. Or, if I could work miracles, maybe all of us triplets. Why not? I would just have to make sure the ship was big enough for us all to have our own space, when needed.

Max sat up and scooted closer to the desk. I wasn't sure what his objective was.

Kathleen continued gathering papers and placing them in the folder. "I'm sending with you a brochure for each trip and a sheet that has all of the pricing options and details. My notes here will be a summary," she said.

Max barked as softly as he could, went to the rack of brochures, pulled one out, and returned it to Kathleen's desk.

Mom came to the edge of her chair and peered over. "That one looks perfect, Max," Mom said. "I want to go to the Mexican Riviera."

Kathleen and I laughed. She got the detail sheet for Max's selection and put it in the folder with the others. "Why don't you take a couple of days and look these over? We can make an appointment for you to return and we can talk about next steps," Kathleen said. She handed Mom the folder.

"I'm ready, Chloe," Mom said.

I stood. "Let's get on Kathleen's calendar before we go," I said. "How about Friday at two p.m.?" I asked Mom.

She was already at the door. "OK, but I've already made up my mind. I want to do the trip that Max picked out," she said.

I turned and looked at Kathleen. "We'll plan to be here Friday at two if that works for you, and we can see about booking that cruise."

Kathleen escorted us to the door. "That sounds great. Thank you for coming in. And Mabel, I think you're going to have the time of your life. You might just get hooked on travel like Donna," she said.

Mom pushed open the door. Max and I followed.

"Thank you." I waved to Kathleen.

CHAPTER NINE

I looked forward to exploring our town's farmer's market today. Max and I would load up on goodies and I got to see my sister Zoe. She and her long-time boyfriend Eldon lived quite far away from town on a little farm that was off-grid. They would bring their haul into town and sell or trade for the supplies they needed. The last time Mom and I had visited Zoe, she had encouraged me to bring Max and stay with them a few days for a respite from the busy times at the hotel. I was getting closer to taking her up on it. Nothing to do and nature for a few days was just what the doctor ordered for Max and me.

The rows of booths lined the perimeter of the library parking lot. It was the largest location in town to be able to house the growing number of vendors. Zoe had a prime location in the middle of the line. The crowd size was growing, and Max and I had to weave through the flow of people to reach Zoe's booth. She was sandwiched between Caroline's Confections and a man that made fishing lures. The nearby lake and ocean fishing was a big industry.

Zoe beamed when she spotted us. That country air agreed with her. She always looked as relaxed as if she had been vacationing on a beach for a few weeks with umbrella drinks. She stepped out from behind the counter and held her arms wide. Max pushed passed me, stepped between us, and looked up at Zoe. "Well, yes. First things first," she said and bent down to embrace Max. They both closed their eyes as they hugged each other. Zoe stood and reached her arms toward me. "Hello, beautiful."

"We need to visit more often if this is how we're treated," I said.

She grabbed my hand and led me into her booth. She swept her arm along the boxes overflowing with every kind of fruit and vegetable we could ever want. "You have your pick of the crop," she said. "I'll get a box started for you." She pulled an empty box from the corner and started filling it with several things. She set it to the side and said, "Why don't you come back here when you're ready to go and pick this up?"

I hugged her. "Thank you, Zoe. That's so generous. What else do you recommend here?" I asked.

"Of course, my neighbor. Caroline has some new candies that she's trying out on us. Her niece is an apprentice at her shop. They melt in your mouth. You have to try them."

Max was snooping through all of Zoe's boxes of produce that were packed into the booth. Zoe got out a yellow squash and held it for him to sniff. He turned his nose up. *That's my boy, no veggies, but bring on the sweets.* I had to disguise healthy for him, but inevitably he picked out the vegetables he didn't like and left them in the bowl. He made his way to a corner box of a small, oblong watermelon. He sniffed and stepped back. He moved to the left side and sniffed again. He stopped for a moment of contemplation. He trotted to the opposite side and sniffed, then pawed it, leaving a little scrape mark on top. He waited. He pawed it again, and waited.

"He thinks it's an animal," I said. He had never seen a watermelon before. "Oh, Max." He looked at me and tipped his head, not sure why his new friend wasn't playing.

"So Zoe, I don't think you'll believe this. Mom and I went to the travel agent's office, and I think she might actually go on a cruise," I said.

"You're kidding! How did you manage that?" she asked. Another customer had arrived and chosen several items. Zoe packed them up and took their payment.

"It's not a done deal yet. I really hope she does," I said.

"That's going to mean you'll be even busier at the hotel. Are you able to handle that?" she asked.

I called Max from behind the counter. Enough of trying to get the watermelon to play with you. "It's only for a short amount of time. And she deserves it. She's worked hard her whole life."

Zoe continued helping customers as we talked. "I heard about the other night at the museum." She shook her head. "I feel so bad for Angela. Joey told me that Angela's a suspect. But we just don't see it."

I shook my head. "Me neither. I'll have to return to the museum and see what I can find out. It's baffled me so far."

"The guy in the booth next door is Bart and Victor's neighbor." Zoe came from around the table and stood inches away from me. She looked around. "He told me he overheard screaming and yelling one night recently, like they were arguing."

I took a step back. "Really?" I asked.

She looked around again and back at me. "Yes, exactly that. Sometimes guys gossip more than women," she said.

"Well, Victor seemed pretty shaken up about the death. I don't think you can fake emotions like he had," I said, remembering the look in his eyes that night at the bingo tournament.

"Maybe," Zoe said. "Something to check out, for sure."

I looked down the row of booths. "I thought I saw him here. Does he have a booth?"

"Yeah, he's somewhere down there. He creates beautiful pieces of art using different types of inlaid wood. I don't think he makes a lot of money with it though."

"Well, Max and I'll wander over there and check it out," I said. I leashed up Max to keep him close to me as we squeezed past the throngs. "We'll stop by on our way out."

Zoe waved and turned to help another customer.

I could see from quite a ways away that Victor had the three walls of his booth filled with the gorgeous designs, but no one was buying them. He spotted me and waved. I returned the gesture.

When we got within earshot, I said, "Hi, Victor."

"Hi, Chloe," he said.

"Your work is stunning."

He sighed. "Yes, I wish more people thought so. I get a lot of lookie loos, and people who say the same thing but don't put their money where their mouth is."

"Well, they're missing out," I said and looked straight into Victor's eyes. "I can't tell you again how sorry I am about Bart."

"I was hoping by coming today and doing something normal, I'd feel better." He bowed his head and shook it. "But I miss having him here with me. It's just not the same."

"I see that you do animals. Would you be able to do a custom piece of Max for me?" I asked.

Victor stepped out from behind the table and looked down at Max. He made a circle around him, evaluating his model. "Well, yes I could. If you get me a photo, that would be best," he said.

I smiled. I was happy to help out an artist. And his work was lovely. "Perfect. I'll be in touch."

"Thank you. And Chloe, thank you for looking into Bart's death. I really am not going to get a moment's peace until his killer is caught."

Max and I turned to retrace our steps to Zoe's booth, gather our box, and head out. Victor seemed genuinely sorrowful at Bart's death. Could he just be putting on a show? Time would tell.

CHAPTER TEN

The crime scene tape cordoning off the dead body and missing collectible was long gone. The only sound in the museum was hushed voices viewing the different displays. Angela had resumed tours while the mystery of her boss's death continued to loom large. Max and I sat on the bench in front of the location where the canteen was supposed to be. If Bart was killed here, I wanted to visualize how it had happened. That might guide me to where I should ask more questions.

Angela had sidled up to me. I jumped when she started talking. "I'm so sorry to startle you, Aunt Chloe," she said.

I stood up and faced her. "No worries. We're all on edge about this." I reached over and hugged her tight. Max jumped down, leaned up against Angela, and looked at her with love. I held her at arm's length and stared into her eyes. "How are you doing?" I asked.

She shrugged and slumped onto the bench. "OK, I guess. I'm so conflicted. I didn't really like Bart. But at the same time, I hope they will consider me for the curator position now that he's gone." She looked up at me, her eyes pleading.

Responding to her unasked question, I said, "I'm trying Angela. It's complicated. Eventually, we'll have answers. Just try to hang in there." I held out my hand. She grasped it and tipped her head down again, beginning to sob. I sat on the bench and put my arm around her.

Out of the corner of my eye, I saw Max slink over to the side table in the display location. He looked all around, in the corners, and then stood on his hind legs with his front feet on the counter. He looked at me, summoning my presence.

I released my arm from Angela and went to see what Max had discovered. At first it wasn't apparent what he saw. I looked at him and shrugged. "What is it?" I asked.

He tapped his paw on a space that, unless you looked closely, you wouldn't notice that it had less dust than the surrounding space. It looked like one of the candlestick holders in the row of six was missing.

I turned around and asked Angela, "How many candle holders should there be on this shelf?" I gestured toward the open space.

She got up from the bench and approached, her brow furrowed. She walked the length of the counter, looking at it from multiple angles. "That's really odd," she said. She moved a few of the other display items, searching for something that obviously wasn't there. She looked up at me and her hand flew to her mouth. "Chloe," was all she could squeak out.

Max got down from the counter and nodded. He had likely just discovered the potential murder weapon.

Angela's eyes darted from me to Max, and to the empty dust-free former location of the missing candlestick. "Let's not get ahead of ourselves," I said, trying to calm myself down as well. "Take a deep breath. I'll alert the police that we have a potential murder weapon. Angela, I need you to go throughout the museum and make sure it didn't make its way elsewhere, and that it is indeed missing."

Her hand dropped to her side and she nodded.

"We're still gathering information. OK?" I said.

She nodded again.

"Can I take a look at Bart's office? Maybe there's something else that might pop up there," I said.

She looked toward the museum entry to see a small group coming into the building. "I have to go, anyway. Yes, please help yourself. And let me know if you need anything else."

I reached down and patted Max, telling him what a great job he did. Now on to explore further.

Bart's office was in the farthest corner of the museum. It was a small eight by eight just big enough for a desk, chair, and filing cabinet. It was highly organized. Pencil holder, stapler, file folders aligned like soldiers. I scanned the area to see if anything felt out of place, perusing one corner at a time. I had hoped not to pry too much, but with everything put in its place, I'd have to scour through drawers. I stepped up to the desk and sat in the chair, again, taking it all in. I started by opening the top left drawer. Trying to disturb as little as possible, I gently lifted the stacks of papers out. I fanned through them to see if something caught my eye. I looked down at Max, and he shook his head.

We continued through the remaining drawers on the left side and moved to the right. Following the same pattern, there was absolutely nothing of interest to guide the investigation of Bart's murder any further. "I don't know, Max. It seems like we're missing something obvious." I opened the bottom right drawer, hoping this last stack of papers held the answers we needed. Or I would even take a clue to more questions, at this point. Something. I looked through each item, hopeful the prize would be at the very end. Nothing. I replaced the papers in the drawer and closed it up. I sat back in the chair, looking around.

Max whimpered. He tilted his head, laser-focused on that bottom right drawer.

"We already looked at that one, buddy," I said. I got up from the desk, ready to leave. Max wasn't budging. "I trust you. Obviously, I'm not having any luck. And you're already batting a thousand for clue discovery today," I said.

He tapped the drawer with his paw. I opened it and retrieved the stack of papers. I began reviewing each one and setting it to the side.

Max barked. He tapped the drawer again.

I returned my attention to the stack and continued moving one piece of paper at a time from right to left.

He bent over and pulled the handle open with his mouth. After the drawer was fully open, he stuck his head all the way in the back and pulled out some crumpled papers. I guess that's an advantage of being eighteen inches off the ground. You've got a great view from down there. He continued pulling out crumpled pieces of paper and placing them in a pile next to me.

I picked one up and pressed it out on the desktop. It was a letter between Bart and Donna. She was reminding them of their deal. With Donna's endorsement of Bart for the position of museum curator, he had agreed to acquire some rare pieces for her personal collection. Well, this certainly confirmed some of the rumors about his shady dealings, but it didn't point to a clue of who would murder him. I continued unfolding the smashed papers to find more letters and a travel brochure.

"Did you find anything useful?" Angela had come into the office.

I grabbed my chest. "You startled me again," I said. My heart raced and my head pounded as I tried to make sense of Max's brilliant discovery. I turned around in the chair to face her. "I'm not sure. Was Bart planning a trip?" I asked.

She came further into the office and picked up the brochure from the desk and looked at it. Then she looked at me. "Not that I know of."

I shoved the entire pile back into the drawer. No sense upsetting Angela any further until I knew for sure what was going on. I had several pieces but I didn't even know if they were to the same puzzle. Max and I had a lot more work to do.

CHAPTER ELEVEN

After our trip to the museum, I needed some time to allow the clues to percolate. I hoped the distraction of creating the decorations for the scholarship auction would be enough of a diversion for my brain. Mom had generously agreed to host the work party if I agreed to pick up the treats. Caroline's Confections and Coffee Shop was our go-to for anything sweet. And Max's favorite place to be spoiled. It bustled on a Friday night. We patiently waited our turn in line. Caroline's display of goodies had significantly grown. There were several new items I had not seen before.

"Hi Chloe," Caroline said as we approached the counter. "I have your box ready to go." She wiped her hands on her apron and turned to retrieve a large box from the back table. "I put a few extra of my newest creation. A cream-filled cupcake. I think it's going to be a big hit." She put the box next to the cash register.

"Thank you," I said. "And I haven't had anything here that hasn't been a hit."

Max knew exactly the routine he needed to perform in order to get a treat. He gently placed his nose on the counter and raised his eyebrows. Caroline came out from behind the displays and placed a treat for Max on the floor. He gently grabbed it with as much politeness as possible, dropped it on the floor, and looked up at me, then Caroline.

She laughed and patted his head. "No fooling him," she said. "I tried a small piece of my new cupcakes, but as always, he's got his heart set on the gingersnaps." She pulled another treat from her apron pocket and placed it on the floor.

He inhaled it and looked up for another.

She held both hands up and rubbed them together to show him there was no more for today.

He tipped his head and returned to my side.

"Chloe, any further progress on Bart's murder?" Caroline asked, and returned to the other side of the counter.

I shook my head. "I wish. It seems the more I ask around, the more complicated it gets. Angela is beside herself that she didn't have anything to do with it. I want to believe her because she's family. But she sure did have a lot of motive. And she was there early the night of the museum unveiling."

"And she's got that sweet daughter too." Caroline packed up additional boxes for more pick-up orders. "Yeah, I can't see it," she said.

"The one I really don't know about is Victor. He and Bart had been overheard in a fight. Couples fight and they normally don't kill each other. But sometimes they do." I grabbed the box of pastries. "We'll just have to keep at it. Thank you for these. Let's go, Max."

He turned to look at me and then back at Caroline.

She put her hand up to the side of her mouth and whispered, "I put a few for him in the box."

I turned and almost smashed my box into the man behind me. "Oh, I'm sorry," I said. "I didn't realize there was anyone behind me."

He stepped to the side to let me pass before I made a total mess of the place. "No worries. Hi Caroline," he said.

"Hi Stan. Have you met Chloe yet?" Caroline asked and pointed my direction.

He bent to give Max's ears a scratch, which prompted a relaxed, happy smile from my pooch. "No, I haven't," he said. "I'd shake your hand, but I don't want to give you another chance to spill your box." He laughed and Max barked. "I think your friend likes me. I'm Stan

York. My brother Paul is doing the construction project at the hotel," he said.

I nodded and gazed at him, seeing a small likeness to Paul. "Ah, OK. Nice to meet you, Stan," I said.

He took a step back. "I won't keep you. I just want to say thank you for Paul's business, which I'm sure he's also said. Ever since Bart canceled our business with the museum, we've both been struggling."

"What do you do?" I asked.

"I'm a party planner. With all of the museum celebrations going on, Bart had been keeping me pretty busy. And after that, Victor canceled the contract for the scholarship presentation. If you or Caroline know of anyone that could use some catering and planning expertise, I'd be forever grateful," Stan said. "I better let you go. Nice to meet you again."

"You too," I said. Max and I turned and headed out the door. Why would Bart and Victor cancel the contracts? Stan and Paul seemed nice enough. And I'm guessing the work was decent. Another direction to pursue for answers.

Donna, Kathleen, and Angela had already arrived at Mom's. We had planned a work session to create all of the decorations for the scholarship presentations happening the next evening. Trixie was already yipping to greet us, mostly Max. She adored him like an older brother. She also pestered him like a little sister. He was a good sport about it and tolerated her tugging his long ears, poking his rear, and generally annoying him. They would get on a roll sometimes and speed around Mom's house like a racetrack.

We entered the house, greeted everyone, and I took the box to the kitchen. I joined the work group in the dining room. Streamers, balloons, posters, and table decorations were spread out on every surface.

"Thank you for bringing those," Mom said.

I took a seat at the table to join the assembly line. "Of course," I said. "Caroline said she put in a few of the new cream-filled cupcakes she made."

"Chloe, why don't you put together the centerpieces?" Mom asked. "We have one here as an example, if you want to do that."

"Mom, I met Paul's brother when I was at Caroline's," I said. I placed seven small bottles in front of me. I grabbed a box with ribbon, glitter, and several sticks with the word "Celebrate" on them. I looked at the example and began assembling the first bottle.

"Stan is so nice," Kathleen said. "I really wish he and Victor had gotten together. But for some reason, Stan also wanted to date Bart."

Kathleen was making table cards and had several stacks already completed.

Max and Trixie had exhausted themselves and joined our work party, plopping down under the dining room table.

"So Donna," Mom began. I looked up at her. She continued her focus on the task in front of her. "I went to see Kathleen. And I think I might go on a cruise with you."

Donna squealed like a little girl. She gave a quiet golf clap. "Mabel, you won't regret it," she said. She sat forward in her chair, waiting for the answer.

Mom continued her task. "Mexico," she said.

More clapping from Donna. "That's fantastic!" She suddenly halted her euphoria and began looking around. "What's that noise?"

We all stopped our work and listened. From under the table came the sound of paper rattling. I thought someone likely had dropped some supplies that the dogs had gotten hold of. I peered under the table and saw Max unwrapping a butterscotch candy. "Oh, Donna. I'm sorry. It looks like Max got into your purse and snuck a candy. He has a relentless sweet tooth," I said.

Donna hauled her bag from under the table and lofted it onto the kitchen counter.

Mom peeked at me and snickered. I couldn't make eye contact with her or I would bust a gut. I'd give just about anything to be a fly on the wall during their cruise. There would be no end to the stories Mom would have when she returned. I couldn't wait.

CHAPTER TWELVE

The layout of the library looked identical to what it was on bingo night. Tables faced the front platform where the presentations would occur. The decorations we had created provided a lovely, festive atmosphere. It would be a wonderful celebration of the graduating high school seniors and a hearty send off for the next phase of their lives.

Mom, Max, and I made our way to the same seats we had during bingo. Each table had several decorations, including blank cards. We were all encouraged to write notes of inspiration to the seniors. The tables quickly filled in with friends and family of the graduates. I looked over the program that had been placed in front of each chair. There would be opening remarks from Judy, of course. Then interspersed, we would be treated to seniors performing in different arts, as well as the scholarship and awards presentations themselves. What a joyous night and a nice break from the stress of the recent tragedy.

"Good evening, everyone." Judy had stepped to the podium to kick us off. "If you will take a seat, we are just about to get started. Thank you," she said. She huddled up with Victor and the high school principal, Mrs. Hardcastle, to review the itinerary. Judy nodded as she reviewed the paper in front of her. She looked at the clock on the wall and returned to the microphone. Victor and Mrs. Hardcastle each took a seat behind Judy on the platform.

"I'd like to welcome you to one of my most cherished events to attend as the mayor of Cedarbrook," Judy began. She scanned the room, taking it all in. After a dramatic pause, she continued, "Tonight we get to celebrate the next class of high school graduates. Please join me in acknowledging their accomplishments." She put her paper down and led us in a round of applause. "And if that wasn't enough, this will be the largest dollar amount of scholarships we've ever given." She grinned big as if she had personally donated the funds. She panned the crowd again.

At that moment, Victor rose and approached Judy's right side, and with a hand to his mouth, whispered in her ear. He dropped his hand and took a step back.

"Are you sure?" Judy asked in a loud whisper. She looked back at the crowd. Her mouth opened and closed without a word. She shook her head. "I'm sorry. I have some disappointing news. I have just been told by the bingo treasurer that we do not, in fact, have the amount of money to award scholarships as I was previously advised."

Victor took another step back toward his chair.

Judy turned to her right, grabbed his arm, and pulled him to the microphone. "You need to tell them how much we have and where the money has gone." She made space for him to address the crowd. A significant amount of mumbling had begun.

From across the room, one of the parents shot out of their seat and yelled, "Where's the money?"

A smattering of other parents stood and another one yelled, "Thief. I think he should be arrested. Call the police."

Victor took a step back from the podium and held his arms up, trying to halt the mob's ire. "Wait a minute. Let me explain," he said.

Those that were standing took their seats. But the low-level grumbling continued.

Victor's shoulders rose and fell. "Yes. I admit it. The funds are not currently there," he said.

The yelling began again, up another octave. Mom leaned over to me and whispered, "This better be good." I agreed. Victor had quite the hole to dig out of, and I didn't see any way he could recover.

"Where are they?" came another shout.

Victor looked at Judy, pleading for her to create some order. She took a step back, leaving him in the arena to fight this out alone.

"He was going to pay them back. I promise. It was just a temporary loan. Bart said no one had to know," Victor said. He voice shook, now caught in the web of deceit.

"Liar," came an accusation from the crowd. "You've been spending a lot of money you don't normally have. Explain that."

Victor shook his head and brought a fist up to his mouth to stifle sobs. He returned to his seat without another word.

Judy returned to the podium and resumed control. She sneered at Victor as he passed by her, and rightly so.

"Well, we're going to have to change up our program tonight. One way or another we will find a way to award the amount in scholarships that was promised," Judy said.

A huge cheer and round of applause roared from the crowd.

Judy beamed. "Before we continue, I'd like to assure you there will be a full accounting of the funds. Victor will no longer manage the books. We'll have a professional look at them from now on," Judy said.

Another huge round of applause and cheers emanated throughout the library, echoing off the walls.

Judy pointed toward me. "I'm sorry to put you on the spot. But, Chloe, would you please take a look at the books and let us know what's really going on?" Judy asked.

What could I say? "Of course. I'd be happy to." Maybe I would get Max to buddy up with me for the task. Together we had become an unbeatable team. I looked over at Max seated between Mom and me. He nodded.

More cheers and calls of "thank you, Chloe" came from the crowd. I smiled, happy to help with anything for the kids. The program for the night continued on, albeit a small deviation from the original plans. The joy of the evening with the smiles on those senior's faces helped us all recover from an inauspicious start to the night. As the evening was wrapping up, Judy reminded everyone to fill out the cards on our tables with words of encouragement for the seniors.

"Chloe, do you have a pen I could borrow?" Mom asked. That woman had the kitchen sink in her purse. How could she not have a pen? I traveled light with a small carry-all just big enough for ID, keys, and money.

"I have one," Angela said as she dug in her purse. She turned and held it out for Mom to take. Max intercepted it just as Mom's hand stretched to take it.

"Max," Mom said. "Give me that."

He clamped down hard, not giving it up. He turned toward me in his chair. I reached to take it out of his mouth and saw the same museum collectible pen Kathleen had at her office. He released it into my hand and looked me straight in the eye. I nodded to acknowledge his message and retrieved the pen for Mom. Was this another piece to the puzzle we were looking for?

CHAPTER THIRTEEN

Paul had arrived for another walkthrough of the hotel expansion project. The Crocus Castle was almost complete and we would get our first look from the inside of the treehouse. Thankfully, Paul had recommended an elevator for this unit. As our tallest building, it warranted an easier lift. Mom, Paul, Max, and I made our way along the path to the farthest location from the office and new lodge. The ground had dried up from a recent rain but remained a bit soft. I would have to remember to ask Paul to firm up the path to this unit with some wood shavings to prevent any slips and falls.

"Be careful, Mom. It's still a bit soft," I said. Thankfully, she relented to wearing a pair of hiking boots I had purchased for her. Those dress shoes she always insisted on wearing were going to land her in a puddle, or worse. I grabbed her hand, just to be safe. We approached the base of the ponderosa pine tree that was the foundation for Crocus Castle. It had grown to a width of almost twenty feet, approaching its size at maturity. Looking up, we could only see the bottom of the wrap-around deck that enveloped the treehouse. The elevator would take us through that and open just outside the front door. My heart palpitated.

"Chloe, why don't I take Mabel up first? Then I'll come back to get you and Max," Paul said.

"Oh, goody," Mom squealed like a giddy schoolgirl. This project for the hotel was making her dream come true. A real legacy left to her recent husband. She had been wanting to do this for so long. I was so pleased I could help make it happen for her.

Paul loaded Mom into the elevator and they slowly lifted off. It was actually quieter than I expected, retaining the tranquility of its surroundings.

Max and I patiently waited for Paul's return. Just as slowly, he descended and opened the gate for us to enter. I looked around and estimated probably four people at the most could fit into this space.

Paul looked over at me and asked, "What do you think?"

"I think it's incredible. Better than I ever imagined," I said.

"Wait until you see the view. I don't want to ruin the surprise for you. But it's spectacular," he said. His excitement was infectious. I bet it was so rewarding to delight your customers with results beyond their wildest dreams.

The elevator came to a halt and Max sped to the opening, anxious to escape. I hadn't even thought about his reaction to that new experience. I hoped it didn't frighten him. He ran down the decking to greet Mom, who stood in the northwest corner taking in the view.

"Chloe, look." She gestured to the tops of the trees as far as the eye could see.

I stopped. My breath, literally taken away. Other than being in an airplane, this was not a view most people would ever see. My marketing brain hummed with ideas for aerial photos. We would have to do it up right for the brochures and website. I continued along the deck toward Mom. "I can just see chairs and a table out here for watching the sunset," I said. "Wow."

Paul chuckled behind us. "I'm guessing you like it so far."

I looked over my shoulder. "It's breathtaking."

Mom pointed to something in the distance. "I can see forever. Look, someone's coming up the road to the hotel." We still had a gravel road to the hotel for the short distance from the main paved highway. It got a little messy during the wet winters.

I stood closer to Mom. "I think that's Donna's car," I said. "We should probably head back to the office. Thanks so much for the tour."

"My pleasure." Paul headed toward the elevator. "Any time. Let's do the same plan as we did when we came up."

Mom got into the elevator with Paul, which left Max and I to wait our turn. When we were all on the ground again, we trekked back to the office.

"That was great, huh Mom?" I asked.

Max took off, sprinting toward Donna. I wasn't sure why he didn't seem friendly toward her, but he must have had a good reason.

We exited the path into the parking lot. Donna had disappeared. "Where did she go?" Mom asked.

"Maybe she went inside," I said. "C'mon Max," I yelled. We turned and headed to the office door.

Max yelped like he had injured himself. I turned around and Donna appeared from the other side of her car. I walked toward her to locate Max. "Hi, Donna. We thought you had already gone inside."

She briskly walked past Mom and me and opened the office door. Over her shoulder she said, "Oh, I dropped something. But I want to talk to you both about a brainstorm I had."

Mom looked at me, shrugged, and followed Donna inside.

I went to investigate what was happening with Max. He emerged from the bushes on the side of the parking lot, limping. Oh no. Every now and then he strained one thing or another after his jaunts. Like a fine-tuned athlete, he periodically needed physical therapy. That usually meant a relaxing massage at Pearl's Pooch Pampering. He stopped where he was and waited. He held his left front paw a few inches from the ground.

"What happened, Max?" I asked. I bent over and began to gently feel up and down his leg to locate the source of the injury. He didn't flinch once. Instead, he held his leg higher so I could see the bottom of his foot. Stuck to his paw was a butterscotch candy. I carefully peeled it off so he could at least walk on it again.

"Max, that sweet tooth is going to get you into deep trouble one of these days," I said. I placed his paw on the ground and headed toward the office. I turned around and saw he hadn't moved from his spot. I walked back toward him and he dove into the bushes. The squirrels had been extremely busy lately, burying food for the winter. Maybe he had located part of their stash. He poked his head out to confirm I was coming and returned into the bushes. OK. I was going to have to follow him to resolve whatever it was he wanted me to see. I parted the branches and followed the sound of rustling.

About six feet in, I saw what he had found. The missing canteen and candlestick holder from the museum. Someone had stashed them in the bushes. I followed him all the way in and picked up the items that were damp from the rains. If not for Max, I don't know that they would have been located for quite a while, if ever.

We wove our way out of the bushes, across the parking lot, and into the office.

CHAPTER FOURTEEN

A s I approached the office door, I spotted Paul coming this way. "Chloe, if you have a few minutes, I have some questions for you and Mabel," he said.

I nodded and slowly opened the office door. Max sprinted past me. I held the door open for Paul and stepped inside.

"Oh, good, Chloe. Donna has a great idea, she wanted—" Mom's jaw dropped open and she stood up. She and Donna had settled into the chairs near the coffee pot. Mom took a step toward me. "What is that? Where did you get it?" she asked.

Max had run to Donna and was now in a tussle with her for her purse. She yanked it hard, but he had a death grip, and there was no way that elderly lady would win that battle. He growled and bared his teeth. She stood and Max tugged hard. Donna lost her balance and the contents of her purse tumbled out, making a pile about a foot tall. At the top of the mound was a giant bag of butterscotch candies.

"Make him stop," Donna screamed.

I stepped further into the office and held out the canteen and candlestick, one in each hand. "Was this what you were looking for in the bushes?" I asked.

"I don't know what you're talking about," Donna said and crossed her arms over her chest. "I came to ask you about hosting a casino night at the new lodge. But this is the thanks I get for trying to help your business?" She stooped and began shoveling the pile of items back into her bag.

Max returned and grabbed the handles of her purse, dragging it to the opposite side of the room.

Donna grabbed her wallet and keys and stood up. "See if I ever help you again. And Mabel? That cruise is off!" Donna yelled and started toward the door.

Paul stepped in front of her, preventing the exit. I didn't think he fully understood what was happening, only that Donna shouldn't be allowed to leave just yet.

"Get out of my way, you big oaf!" Donna tried to skirt around Paul, but he stepped into her path.

I put the canteen and candlestick on the counter and wiped my grimy hands on a towel. "Donna," I uttered quietly, trying to defuse the situation. "I read the letters between you and Bart. I know you were blackmailing him to get those museum pieces for your personal collection." I took a small step toward her. I kept my voice low. "And your muddy shoes from the other day were because you were trying to find where you had ditched the items the previous time you were here," I said.

She turned toward me. "Bart was always so full of himself. He wouldn't have had that position if it weren't for me. I knew more about collectibles than he ever would," she said. Her chin trembled. Her arms went limp.

I took a step toward her. "What happened, Donna?"

She looked at me and we both shuffled back toward the chairs. I continued in lockstep to keep her moving. I gestured to the chair. She sat, bent over, and began weeping into her hands.

Paul brought over a box of tissues, and I handed them to Donna. I made the signal and mouthed to Paul to call the police. He nodded. I needed to keep Donna talking until they arrived. "It's all over, Donna," I said.

Mom joined the conversation after the shock of the situation had dissipated. "Now what am I going to do? I've already put down a deposit on that cruise that's non-refundable," she said. She sat down in a huff next to Donna.

I stood guard. "We'll figure something out, Mom. Don't worry. I'm sure Kathleen can help us," I said.

Max joined us, still dragging Donna's empty purse like a prized catch, prancing to Mom's side. He whimpered, dropped the purse, and looked up at Mom. She reached down and patted his head.

"I'm so sorry, Mabel," Donna said, looking at Mom with pleading eyes.

"You should be apologizing for Bart," Mom said.

Donna took a handful of tissues and dabbed her drippy eyes and nose. "Mabel, I don't know what'll happen to my collection."

Mom stood, faced Donna, and jammed her hands onto her hips. "That's what got you into this pickle in the first place, your obsession with those things. And your collection isn't nearly as nice as all of the pieces we have here." Mom was not relenting.

Donna pleaded with Mom. "I know. That's why I want you to take care of what I have. Mabel, you and your family care as much about the history of Cedarbrook as anyone. I can't think of a better home for my babies until I can see them again."

Mom scoffed. "You got that right," she said and walked over to Paul. "Paul, do you think we could expand the plans for the display case we had?" she asked.

"Of course, Mabel. Anything for you," he said.

Mom strutted back to Donna and said, "There. All taken care of. Donna, if you weren't so full of yourself, maybe this wouldn't have happened. Your gambling habit just went too far this time. And poor Bart had to pay the price." Mom read her the riot act. It was reminiscent of the scolding we kids used to get at home. Donna would probably be relieved when the police came to take her away. She slumped further into the chair.

Max tiptoed to the pile of Donna's purse contents, trying to go unnoticed. He poked his nose searching for treats. "Max," I whispered. He paused, then continued prodding. "Max," I repeated.

I grabbed the purse and loaded the stuff back inside. He deserved the biggest gingersnaps I could find. It might take a special order at Caroline's to make him all that he should get for finally cracking this case wide open. He looked up at me, as if reading my mind, and smiled from ear to ear. His little tail took off again like that helicopter, happy for a job well done.

CHAPTER FIFTEEN

We were finally at the stage of the hotel construction project where we were confident enough to plan the grand re-opening. I was always in favor of going to the experts for help for things I don't know. Today, Mom, Max, Stan, Caroline, and I were all in the back room at Caroline's Confections. Caroline had set out samples of all the treats we might order for the event. Four tables were covered with every kind of sweet you could imagine, many I had never seen in her display cases.

"Caroline, you have really outdone yourself. This looks incredible," I said as I toured the tables. "How will we be able to narrow it down?" I laughed. We all circled the desserts several times and then gathered at a table to commence the planning.

Stan sat between Mom and me. He reached out a hand to each of us and looked back and forth. His voice cracked. "Chloe and Mabel, how can I ever pay you back with my gratitude? I owe you for so many things," he said.

I smiled. "I'm just glad we found you to help us plan this shindig. We want to do it up right," I said. Stan's party-planning business had begun to recover. The contract for the bingo games had even been restored.

He released our hands and opened the notebook in front of him. "Well, then you've come to the right place. Caroline and I will knock it out of the park. This town owes you for solving Bart's murder and finding the missing museum piece, even if it was damaged," he said.

"That Bart was a scoundrel," Mom interjected.

Max jumped up and started barking. He sauntered over to Caroline and placed his head on her thigh, opening his eyes wide. The two of them had become thick as thieves.

Caroline looked at me for permission. "He can have whatever he wants," I said. "If he hadn't been nosing around those bushes and got that candy stuck to the bottom of his paw, we might still be trying to figure out what happened."

Caroline knew Max well and always treated him right. She had a plate of his favorite gingersnaps in the middle of the table. She retrieved one, showed it to him, and tossed it up. He caught it mid-air, like the well-tuned athlete he was. He sat and stared at her, encouraging her to keep them coming. "OK, boy. Let's pace ourselves. We've got a lot to cover in our meeting," Caroline said and turned back to our planning committee. Max laid down beside her, still fixated on her hand the moment it had another treat inside of it.

"I'm still shocked that Donna did it." Mom joined the conversation. "I mean, she's a little old lady," she said. Mom didn't think of herself as a little old lady. That was partially why she was still able to help run the hotel at age eighty.

"I don't think she planned it. Since she used that candlestick to bonk him on the head, I'm guessing it just happened in the heat of the moment. Even so, she's still guilty," I said.

"It's still really sad. Bart didn't deserve that," Caroline said.

"Well, at least Angela was able to bail them out at the museum. That girl knows her history." Mom huffed. "She should have gotten the position in the first place."

The museum board, minus Donna, unanimously voted to hire Angela as the curator. She got the same compensation deal as Bart. The more business she brought in, the higher percent of commission she would earn. She had already planned the events for the next year, outdoing Bart. Plus, I think her infectious personality and authenticity drew people to the place. It has gotten to be one of the busiest locations in town.

So many people's lives had been upended because of Donna's deed. I hoped now that she had been caught, we could begin to heal. With Angela moving out of Victor's, he had moved in with his sister, Kathleen. The judge gave him community service hours for being complicit in taking the bingo money. He seemed repentant and was trying to build up his art business.

Caroline got up and handed out plates to everyone. "Why don't we sample these as we're doing our planning?" she asked. "There's a lot to try."

She must have prepared at least twenty-five different items. We all got up and shopped around to choose a few to begin our tasting. When we resumed our seats, Max circled the tables several times, waiting for his share of the goodies. Caroline place two more gingersnaps on a napkin and put it on the floor. Max inhaled those and looked around for the next course of his meal.

"That's enough for now, Max." He dutifully laid down. "Caroline, these truffles melt in your mouth," I said with my mouthful. "And the little crunch inside is delicious."

"Those are the newest creation. My niece Haley is an apprentice with me for the next year. She's really brought a lot of new ideas from her training at the culinary institute," she said.

I plopped another truffle in my mouth. "Your generosity to make up for the stolen bingo money was above and beyond."

"Well, with my business doing so well," Caroline said, "I wanted to give back. There was a time I wasn't sure I would be able to continue. But thanks to everyone rallying around me, we're finally operating in the black."

"I'm sure those students and their parents are extremely grateful," I said.

"Mmmmm," Mom mumbled. I looked over and her entire plate was empty. Stan, Caroline, and I looked at each other and smirked. "What?" Mom asked. "Caroline said to try them. I'm just following instructions." She got up to refill her plate. She returned to the table and said, "I hope this celebration will be one that people talk about for a long time." Mom looked at me. "Chloe, did you tell them?"

I held my hands up. "I thought you should be the one to share the good news," I said.

Caroline and Stan looked at each other.

"Does this mean—" Stan started. He covered his mouth.

"No, Stan. I'm still working on that," Mom said. "Chloe just doesn't know it yet."

I picked up a cookie and took a bite, averting my eyes from everyone. "Mom, stop trying to fix me up. When I'm good and ready, I'll search for a boyfriend by myself." My cheeks were on fire.

"Harrison and his family are coming for a visit when we have the grand re-opening. I get to see my son and have my family together again," Mom said. She beamed. This had been her wish for so long.

Caroline reached out a hand. "Mabel, I'm so happy for you."

"That's wonderful," Stan chimed in. "Now I get to do my job and make this an epic party." He looked at me and winked. "And Mabel, you and I will strategize later."

"Yes, we will, Stan," Mom said.

Max returned to the conversation, barking and wagging his tail. It would be an epic party, indeed.

NEXT RELEASE - MISTLETOE AND MISFORTUNE

E pic plans are underway to celebrate the hotel's glorious expansion. But the untimely death of a pompous chef right in the middle of the preparations might be what closes down the hotel for good. Ben's award-winning restaurant and food are legendary, but not as much as his arrogance and unscrupulous dealings.

As Chloe and Max work to salvage the event, they discover secrets about the chef that will crack the case wide open. When Ben's wife takes the helm of the business with suspiciously no remorse for his death, she jumps to the top of the list of suspects.

The shocking clues that come to light will entangle Chloe's family, her mother's livelihood, and culminate with a bombshell that will leave everyone dumbfounded. Can Chloe and Max connect the dots in this culinary conundrum before the hotel doors are shuttered for-

ever in ***Mistletoe and Misfortune***?

Scan the QR code below with your device's camera to order now.

ABOUT THE AUTHOR

Sue Hollowell is a wife and empty nester with a lot of mom left over.
Not far from her everyday thoughts are dreams of visiting tropical
locations. She likes cake and the more frosting the better!
Scan the QR code below with your device's camera to follow her
author page on Facebook.

Printed in Great Britain
by Amazon